Meant to Be

Meant to Be

A Four Irish Brothers Winery Romance

Nan Reinhardt

TULE
PUBLISHING

Dedication

For Moe and Har, with love. Great friends and the best betas ever. Thank you for your honest feedback and your unwavering support.

Chapter One

MEGAN MACKENZIE PLOPPED down in the booth at Mac's Riverside Diner, raked her fingers through her blond curls, and grinned at Samantha Hayes. "Please tell me you ordered me some coffee."

"I did. Norma's brewing a fresh pot as we speak, just for you, Madam Mayor." When Sam returned the smile, Megan was struck for the hundredth time in five months at how quickly they had become good friends. "I also ordered us both a slice of lemon meringue pie because I followed Paula in here and it looks amazing."

"You are my queen." Megan bowed her head and waved a hand in front her face in a mock gesture of servitude.

"These occasional afternoon girl-talk breaks are exactly what I need." Sam blew a breath that ruffled her auburn bangs. "I adore Harry, but good Lord, his file system—and I'm using the term loosely here—is a disaster. I had to get out of there today before I just put a match to the whole place."

"That bad, eh?" Megan nodded thanks to Norma as the server placed steaming mugs of coffee and slices of pie in front of them. She had to agree with Sam about the afternoon breaks. They'd begun meeting at the Riverside a couple of days a week not long after Sam had moved down from Chicago right after Christmas. It was a perfect opportunity for them to get to know each other and cement the friendship that started when Megan's good friend Conor Flaherty had fallen in love with Samantha Hayes.

Megan had realized Sam and Conor belonged together the first time she'd seen them in the same room. They couldn't keep their eyes off each other, and Meg had been delighted that after much sorrow, Conor was finally starting to live again, thanks to Samantha. Now Sam was fast becoming a fixture in River's Edge, having taken over Harry Evans's law practice when Harry decided to run for circuit court judge.

"Worse!" Sam took a sip of coffee. "And, bless his heart, he's got the old dining room that has always been his conference room filled with campaign stuff, so I have nowhere to sort things out. Every time I suggest tossing even a single piece of paper, Alice nearly has heart failure." She leaned in. "I've been sneaking boxes up to my apartment after she leaves at night and going through them."

"How long are you required to keep files?" Megan closed her eyes in ecstasy at the first lemony bite of pie.

Paula Meadows made the best pies in town, everyone agreed, which was why Meg's dad, Mac, bought them to serve at the Riverside rather than making his own. A gourmet chef, her dad could whip up amazing desserts at the drop of a hat, but he'd chosen to focus his efforts on cooking meals. He still baked his own baguettes, but he bought his desserts and pastries from Paula's Bread and Butter Bakery. It was a fine arrangement for both of them and something Megan was grateful for every time she paid Paula's monthly invoice.

"Five years after termination of representation according to the state of Indiana and there's the rub." Sam licked a bit of meringue off her upper lip. "Most of his clients have been his clients since… forever!"

"Man, that makes it hard to discard paperwork."

"I'm trying to convince Alice that we can scan most files and save them electronically—perfectly legal and acceptable. She's balking, but seriously, how many bankers' boxes can one office maintain? I swear there are files in there from when Harry started the practice in 1970. I love her. She's got a mind like a steel trap and she can recall any case he's ever had in scary detail, which makes her invaluable to me. But she and I are going to have to come to terms with who is the attorney and who is the secre—whoops, I mean, *office manager*."

Megan had an idea. "Is the basement in that old place dry?"

"I dunno. I've never been down there." Sam eyed her curiously. "Why?"

"If it's a dry basement, why not hire a couple of kids from the high school to build you some storage down there?

You could set up those steel office shelving racks that libraries and museums use and put all the boxes down there in some kind of order. We did that with the records in city hall two years ago and every summer, I hire some students to scan stuff. It's working out great. I know you can't let kids scan legal documents, but once you're organized downstairs, you can slowly introduce Alice to scanning. I doubt you'd have to scan every single document in the place. I'll bet you can take his current client list and just do theirs for now. Get them into the computer so you can work with their files and cases, then figure out the rest after Harry wins the election and that office becomes yours for keeps."

Megan hoped she wasn't jinxing either Harry's chances at becoming circuit court judge or Sam's at taking over his practice for good by saying that. Probably not—Harry had already won the primary and his opponent on the other side was the current judge—a woman who had been on the bench way too long, in Meg's humble opinion. Since no one was running against Megan for mayor of River's Edge this year, she was helping stump for Harry, knocking on doors, passing out literature, and making sure everyone in town had a ride to their polling place come November. She knew, without any conceit at all, that having the mayor behind him was a boost to Harry's campaign.

"That's a good idea. I'll check out the basement when I get back today." Sam scraped the last of her pie from the plate and popped it in her mouth with a satisfied sigh.

"Enough of my whining. Life is fabulous, Conor is amazing, Ali's adorable, and the wedding plans are coming along great. That's me. I'm dying to hear about your date Sunday. How'd it go?"

Megan leaned one elbow on the table and rested her chin on her palm. "Where to begin?" She rolled her eyes, then chuckled at Sam's disappointed expression.

"Really?" When Sam folded her arms across her chest and scowled, Meg couldn't help laughing out loud.

"Honestly, Sam, you're more into in this whole internet dating thing than I am, and I'm the one doing it."

"I just keep hoping the right guy will come along. You deserve a wonderful man… someone like Conor."

Meg just shook her head. "There's only one Conor and he's pretty well sewn up."

"That he is." Sam sighed dreamily. "Okay, what happened?"

As much as she loved Sam for her concern, Megan wasn't all that worried about finding a man. She enjoyed being single, even at the ripe old age of thirty-seven. She liked the freedom that came from having no one to answer to except Mamie Eisenhower, her big yellow cat. If she wanted nothing more than cheese and crackers for supper, Mamie didn't insist she cook a full meal. When she took a notion to ride her bike along the river on a Saturday afternoon, Mamie happily stayed home and slept in the sun. If she had to work late or had meetings to attend every night one week or events where she had to make a mayoral appearance, Mamie never complained one bit.

Mamie didn't mind Meg's trips to Paris each spring and fall to visit her mother, as long as someone came in every day to feed her and clean out her litter box. Mamie never groused about Meg's shoe addiction, her love of sappy romantic comedies, or her penchant for riding her red bicycle everywhere right up until late November turned to bitter winter. And okay, sometimes she got lonely and restless, but all in all, life was good. At least that was what she kept telling herself.

From the expectant look on Sam's face, she wasn't going to let this go, so Meg sat back. "Well, right off, he was gorgeous and he knew it. Plus, he was kind of a jerk about the fact that I wouldn't meet him at the gambling boat in Vevay."

"Eww." Sam's nose wrinkled in disgust.

"I know, right?" Meg agreed with a brisk nod that brought several blond curls into her eyes. She brushed them away. "Not that I don't like a trip to the boat, but I didn't want to go gambling on a first date. So we met at Conor's tasting room in town. I figured we could taste some wine, have a cheese and fruit tray, and I'd be someplace where people know me so if he got handsy, I'd have backup. Char opened the deck this weekend, it was a beautiful day, and she and Chris were pouring, so there was my protection."

"Makes perfect sense. What else went wrong?"

"Everything. He made fun of Big Red, he—"

Sam held up one hand. "Wait. He made fun of your bike? The beautiful bike Sean bought you for Christmas last year?"

"Yes, three speeds, coaster brakes, and a painted basket on the front apparently are not as cool as his vintage Mustang, which he could *not* quit talking about. He actually opened the hood to show me the engine."

"Oh, dear Lord."

"Yes. Then he dissed every one of Conor's wines, telling me that it was a shame that 'Hoosiers have such a tragically immature palate.'" Meg air-quoted the end of the sentence. "However, that didn't stop him from drinking nearly an entire bottle of pinot all by himself while we sat out on the deck."

"Okay, I hated him for the Big Red thing, but now I really despise him!" Sam slapped her palm on the Formica surface of the table.

Meg held up one finger. "It gets worse."

"Impossible!"

"He kept staring at me with this... this *weird* look on his face. Finally, I asked him if I had something on my cheek or in my teeth. I did dig into that summer sausage that Char puts on the cheese plates. Man, that stuff is good!"

"What did he say?" Sam's tone was cautious.

"He got this disappointed look and said, 'You looked smaller in your picture'."

"What?" Sam practically levitated from her seat.

"He said he usually doesn't date anyone bigger than a size six, although sometimes he'll go out with an eight if she's tall and can pull it off." Meg snorted a laugh, but Sam didn't even crack a smile. As a matter of fact, Meg could almost see steam rising from her friend's ears.

"Are you kidding me?"

Megan sighed. "Oh, how I wish I was."

"What did you say? Please tell me you told him to go straight to hell."

Meg grinned. "Actually, I stood up and said, 'Then you are right out of luck with my size fourteen butt, aren't you, big boy?' and I shook my booty at him and marched into the winery."

The incident wasn't one bit painful, which surprised Meg. Although her curves were no problem for her, it did sometimes bother her that other people found them less than attractive. She'd been curvy nearly all her life—something she inherited from her dad's side of the family where all the women were sturdy Scottish stock. Her mother was a svelte Parisienne, who, even at fifty-nine, still complained about her own flat boyish figure and coveted Meg's rounded hips and full breasts.

"Dang, I wish I'd been there. I'd have let the air out of those Mustang tires!" Indignation laced Sam's tone. "Please tell me he left."

"He did, but not before he stopped me as I was getting

on my bike to ask me if he could call me again."

"Oh, honey." Sam shook her head, her expression waffling between disgust and sadness. "I'm so sorry."

Meg waved her concern aside. "Pfft. Don't be. I'm not. He was a douchebag. I knew it before he ever mentioned my ass."

"Your ass is gorgeous, so screw him," Sam declared as Norma stopped by with the check.

She laid the small black folder on the table. "I'm supposed to tell you two when your hour is up. It's up and it's your turn to pay, Meg, although why either of you pay here is beyond me." She turned away, then glanced over her shoulder and winked. "Oh, and by the way, I agree completely. As asses go, yours is quite respectable. And I'm not just saying that because you're the boss's daughter and the mayor. Unquestionably, you've got a cute tush on you."

Meg grinned. "For that, she gets a 75 percent tip." She took up the folder and shoved several bills into it.

"Why *do* you pay here? You own the place." Sam's perfect brows furrowed. "I've wondered that, but I keep forgetting to ask you."

Meg raised one finger in admonition, before giving her a smile. "*Dad* owns the place. But as his bookkeeper, it's just cleaner if everyone pays. You know what they say, *there's no such thing as a free lunch.*"

Sam chuckled. "Or a free piece of pie? Makes sense— next time is on me."

NAN REINHARDT

Meg nodded, then sighed. "Sam, I think I'm off the dating sites for a while. Eight truly bad dates in as many weeks? I need a break, sister."

"Okay." Sam gathered up her lightweight jacket as Meg rose and shrugged into hers. "I'll stop pushing."

"Thank you."

Sam's cell phone sang Ed Sheeran's "Perfect" and her eyes lit up. "Ah, speaking of fabulous dates—it's Conor."

Meg gave her no-kidding look. "As if I couldn't tell. Ed Sheeran? Seriously? Jeez, you really are sappy in love, aren't you?"

Sam nodded, her lips curved in a shamelessly happy grin. "One second." She held up a hand. "Hey, babe, what's up?" Her expression sobered as she listened intently. "Oh, dear God," she moaned into the phone and Megan's curiosity exploded.

"What?" Megan whispered, fear clutching in her belly. Something bad had happened. Was it Ali? Had the child gotten hurt at preschool?

Sam shook her head slightly, her face grim. "Yes, yes, go… now. Char and I can handle things here. I'll get Ali from school and stay with her at the house. Leave her car seat in the winery for me and put a sign on the door that you're closed for the rest of today. Char will know who to call to help out while you're gone. It'll be fine. Do you want me to call the firm and see if I can get some more details?"

Meg's heart dropped to her socks and then rose in her

throat. *Oh, no! Sean!* Something had happened to Sean in Chicago. Something awful from the horrified look on Sam's face and the fear that shook her voice.

"Well, if you talked to Charlie Smith, then you've got as much information as I could ever get." Tears welled in Sam's brown eyes. "You're meeting Bren and Aidan at O'Hare? Okay. Drive safe, love. If he's in surgery, you've got plenty of time to get there." She listened for a moment. "I know, I know. But please be careful—you won't be any use to Sean if *you're* in a wreck. Call me as soon as you know anything." She listened again. "I love you, too." She tapped the screen and turned to Megan, tears rolling down her cheeks.

Meg was afraid to ask, but she did anyway. "What happened?"

"Sean's been shot." Sam crumpled back into the booth, sobbing.

Megan gasped as bile rose in her throat. She couldn't even comprehend Sam's words. Sean was *shot*? The invincible Sean Flaherty? Her buddy? Her best friend? His handsome face flashed into her mind—the lock of dark hair that invariably fell across his brow, the blue, blue eyes that sparkled sapphire with wit or turned dark navy with emotion, that killer smile, those amazing Flaherty dimples… *impossible!*

"What?" She sat down across from Sam. *"Shot?"* She could hardly catch her breath. "When? Where?"

Sam grabbed a napkin from the dispenser on the table

and swiped at her eyes. "I–I don't know much. Charlie Smith at the firm said it happened right outside the courthouse in Evanston early this afternoon. Some crazy woman. The wife of his current client. They took him to Northwestern; he's in surgery right now." She took a shaky breath. "Conor's driving up to meet Aidan and Brendan at the airport, then they're heading to the hospital." She covered her mouth with both hands as if that could stop her lips from trembling, then shuddered. "Dear God, Meg."

Megan closed her eyes, trying desperately to banish the dreadful pictures in her head—Sean on a gurney, pale and bleeding—and replace them with ones from the last time she'd seen him—grinning and pouring sparkling wine on New Year's Eve.

They'd hugged each other at midnight because neither of them had had a date, and Sean had pressed his warm lips to her forehead. "You're the best, Megs," he'd murmured and held her close to his brawny chest for a long moment. She felt the even beat of his heart under the navy sweater he wore—the one she'd knitted for him for Christmas that made his eyes look deep blue.

"I'm going up there." Megan stood and gazed at Sam. "I *have* to, Sam. He's my oldest and dearest friend. Maybe there's nothing I can do, but I can spell the guys at visitation and maybe, I dunno, give blood or something. I just know I can't stay here. I'll go crazy. I *have* to see him."

Sam stared at her silently, then sighed. "Come on. Let's

trade cars. I don't trust your old beater to make it to Indian-apolis, and you sure as heck can't ride Big Red all the way to Chicago."

Chapter Two

S EAN CRACKED ONE eye open ever so slightly, but saw only an unfamiliar white ceiling and a dimmed light fixture, so he shut it again. His head throbbed, his leg and shoulder both hurt like hell, and his mouth was dry as dust. And he was cold, so unbelievably cold, in spite of the blanket covering him. He shivered.

Where am I?

The room was shadowed and the faint odor of disinfectant permeated the atmosphere around him. He moved his right hand over an inch or two, which sent a sear of pain to his shoulder. But he felt a metal bar.

A hospital bed? I'm in the hospital?

His right leg was up in the air and it ached when he tried to move it. A sudden whirring sound above him nearly took the top of his head off while a vise gripped his left arm. And was someone snoring next to him? He listened. No, not snoring, just snuffling slightly. Panic set in.

What the hell?

Through sheer force of will, he opened his eyes, both of them this time. It took every ounce of strength he had to turn his head and blink. When his vision cleared, he was shocked to see Megan Mackenzie curled up in a chair so close he could reach out and touch her—if he'd been able to move his damned right arm.

Megs? The word wouldn't transfer from his brain to his lips, so he tried once more. Something sounding more like a sick frog croaking came out, but she woke with a start and turned her knock-your-socks-off brandy-colored eyes on him. Then she smiled and suddenly, he was safe again. Warmth flooded his whole body and the fear that had settled in his belly when he first tried to open his eyes diminished just a little.

"Hello there." Her voice was husky with sleep and she stretched, pulling her legs out from under her and rising to stand next to his bed. "You're awake finally."

He tried again to speak, but couldn't get words over his dry tongue, so she reached behind her for the pitcher of ice water that sat on the nightstand.

"Okay if I sit you up a little bit?" she asked even as she touched the button on the remote lying next to him on the bed. She filled a glass, tore open a straw, and offered it to him with a grin. "Hey, look, big guy, bendy paper straws, just like we had back in fifth grade."

While Meg held the glass, Sean took a long sip of water, allowing the icy liquid to slide down his scratchy throat. *Heaven!* When he'd drunk his fill, he turned his head away. "Thanks." He was still croaky, but not as bad as before. "What day is this?"

"Tuesday." Meg set the glass aside and brushed gentle fingers over his forehead.

Sean swallowed and his voice cleared a bit more. "What the hell happened?"

Meg's lips curved up and he felt that smile all the way to his toes, which he'd been secretly moving, doing a full body check to make sure everything was still where it belonged and worked. As far as he could tell, all his parts were functional, except his right leg. That appendage was encased in a hard cast and hanging from a traction device, while his right shoulder, which burned like hellfire had a giant bandage on it. He could move the toes that stuck out of the cast and when he tried to lift the leg, his hip joint worked.

"You were shot, dude." Meg interlaced her fingers with his, and that felt wonderful, until he moved his shoulder and sent another shaft of pain through it.

Dammit.

He adjusted his body, moving slowly to pull himself a little higher on the pillow, a trick what with all the tubes and monitors.

"Hang on, Sean. Let me help you." Meg released his hand, then slid her arm under his back, below his shoulders, and fluffed the pillows there before raising the head of the bed a bit more.

Finally sitting up as comfortably as he could, given that he was in freaking *traction*, he gazed up at her. "*You're* here." The confusion was lifting, but he needed her to fill in the blank spaces.

"Where else would I be?" Meg pulled the chair closer to his bed, sat, and reached between the bars to lay one hand on his arm. "I drove up yesterday after Conor called Sam."

"I'm glad," Sean replied and suddenly a lump formed in his throat and tears stung his eyelids. No. No way was he going to cry, even if that was all he wanted to do. He swallowed hard. "I got shot? Who shot me?" Unbelievable he had no memory of what had happened to him in the last twenty-four hours.

"Some crazy lady, apparently." Meg eyed him as he tried not to wince. "You're in pain. Let me get the nurse."

"No." He took her fingers again. "Not yet. Just let me get clear." He reached his left hand across to touch her cheek. "What time is it? Have you been here all night?"

"It's a little after seven in the morning." She jerked her head toward the clock on the wall behind her and squeezed his fingers. "Your brothers are here, too. I sent them down to get some breakfast. Bren needed caffeine."

"It's a little early for Brendan if he doesn't have coffee," Sean agreed, closing his eyes and letting his head drop against the pillows. "Shot where?"

"The surgeon said one bullet went right through your shoulder, missed the bone and went out. So you have muscle damage that will heal rather quickly. The one in your thigh shattered your femur, but—"

"Shattered?" He gasped and opened his eyes wide. *Shat-*

tered did not sound good, not good at all. "What—what does that mean?"

"Take it easy." She rose and ran one soft hand over his cheek and smoothed the hair away from his brow. "He said you were lucky it didn't hit the femoral artery. You'd have bled to death in two minutes. Right there on the courthouse steps."

"Somehow, not feeling too lucky here." He tried to move his right leg, but the traction prevented him. "Will I… will I walk again?"

"Yes, of course." Meg nodded and grinned. "You don't think a mere bullet could keep your ass down, do you? There's a titanium rod in your thigh and some pins and God knows what else—a bunch of hardware. You're practically bionic, my friend. You've got some PT ahead of you and you may not ever run a marathon, but you'll sure be dancing with me at Conor and Sam's wedding."

"Are you sugarcoating this, Megan?" Sean asked. She was too chipper. It was creeping him out.

"I'm telling you what the surgeon told us last night." She patted his chest. "It's me. I wouldn't lie to you just to make you feel better, even though you do look like hammered crap right now."

"Thanks a ton." He chuckled, then winced. "No, you wouldn't." He could always depend on Megan to tell him the unvarnished truth—she'd been doing it since fifth grade when she told him his feet were too big for his body after she'd tripped over them on the school bus. Fortunately, he grew into his feet and into a friendship with Megan that had remained strong since that fateful day so many years ago.

"Are you hungry?"

"I don't know." He thought about it and couldn't decide. Too much was going on in his body right now—pain signaled from his chest and his leg and the damn blood pressure cuff was squeezing the heck out of his bicep again. His head was pounding and a monitor above him started beeping.

Meg hit the call button. "It's time to get a pro in here." She dropped a quick kiss on his cheek and strode to the door, looking both ways down the hall.

Sean was too tired and in too much pain to argue with her, plus he really, *really* had to pee, but things down there didn't feel quite normal either.

A brawny male nurse bustled in. "Well, look who finally decided to join us." He gave Sean a quick wink and logged into a computer that was on a swing-arm near the bed. "Hi, Mr. Flaherty, I'm Colt, your nurse for the next"—he glanced at his watch—"um, looks like nine and half hours. Let's see what's going on." He tapped whatever monitor was beeping and stopped the noise, bringing Sean's headache down to about a level eight. "Where are you on the topic of breakfast, my friend?" Colt gazed at the computer, then fiddled with a couple of the monitors. "Doc says liquid diet today, probably soft food tomorrow. After that, you're wide open for anything at all from our lovely hospital cuisine. Seriously, they do good food here."

"Coffee?" Sean croaked hopefully, glancing over at Megan, who leaned against the doorjamb, clearly trying to stay out of the nurse's way. He dropped his voice to a gravelly whisper. "And I need to... you know..." He nodded to the en suite bathroom.

"Pee?" Colt chirped as he checked Sean's shoulder bandage. "You've got a catheter, dude, so that's all handled for you."

Heat rose from Sean's neck into his cheeks and he swiped a hand over his mouth and jaw. "TMI, Colt," he muttered through gritted teeth.

Megan giggled. "I think I'll just step out for a second." She gave Sean a little wave. "I'll be right out here in the hall."

Sean closed his eyes and shook his head. "Sure, okay," he said, giving up on any pretense of privacy or decorum, even though Colt did jerk a curtain around the bed before tossing the covers off the lower half of his body.

MEGAN LEANED AGAINST the wall outside Sean's room and closed her eyes, willing the hospital sounds and smells away. She really hated hospitals. Had ever since she'd watched her grandfather die in one when she was sixteen. And seeing her best buddy all bandaged and hooked up to IVs and machines and wires and pulleys was almost too much to bear, although the surgeon had assured them he would recover fully.

She'd met the other three Flaherty brothers in the surgery waiting room the night before, just as Dr. Clark appeared, his green scrubs wrinkled and sweat-stained and his dark skin shiny with the exertion of the long surgery to repair Sean's leg. He was clearly exhausted, but he sat with them in a private conference room and detailed the ORIF surgery—*open reduction and internal fixation*. She'd written it down. In fact, Megan had taken detailed notes as the surgeon had explained all he'd done to put Sean's shattered thigh back together. It was how she coped—the CPA in her simply compartmentalized every situation. Get the facts, sort them out, research what she needed to do, and then deal.

Sean's brothers had asked a million questions and Dr. Clark sat patiently answering every one. Conor wanted to know how soon they could take him home. Dr. Clark explained that Sean would spend about five days in the hospital, then be transferred to a rehab facility on the hospital campus for about another week so the surgeon could keep an eye on his progress. He would need extensive rehabilitation for several months, so Meg had jotted a note to research outpatient rehabs back home. Clearly, Sean's brothers were expecting to take him home to recover. He had no family in Chicago, and there was no way the Flahertys would leave one of their own to cope all alone in the city. Nope, no doubt about it, Sean was going back to River's

Edge, at least for a while.

Brendan worried about PTSD—didn't shooting victims suffer from psychological trauma? *How can we help him with that?* Dr. Clark assured them Sean would be evaluated by a psychologist while he was in the hospital. Meg made another note to talk to Lianne Morrison, a classmate from college, who was now a psychologist and therapist at St. Mark's Hospital down home.

Aidan wondered about a scar and would his big brother be gimpy the rest of his life. Dr. Clark had grinned tiredly, his dark eyes sparkling. He might have a limp when he was extremely tired, but with physical therapy, exercise, and hard work, Sean should make a full recovery. Meg had immediately thought about riding the bike paths along the Ohio River and hiking the trails in the state park just north of town. She could help him exercise outdoors this summer and on rainy days, they'd hit the workout room at the high school or maybe Tierney Ashton's yoga classes. She'd written *yoga stretches* in her notebook.

So many details to work out, but the most important thing was that her dear friend was going to be okay. Tears burned her eyelids and slid down her cheeks as she rested her head against the cool tile wall. Visions of what could have happened if the bullet to his leg had hit his femoral artery, if the one in his shoulder had struck his lung or his heart... Dear God, she'd have lost him forever.

"Hey?" A deep voice interrupted her tangled thoughts

and when she opened her eyes, the most beautiful man she'd ever seen peered down at her. He was *beautiful*—there was no other word. Even through blurry tears, he was incredible looking. "Can I help?" He offered a neatly folded, white handkerchief—an actual cloth handkerchief.

She blinked and stared at him for a moment, unable to tear her eyes away from that perfect face. Black hair tumbled across his forehead and over his collar, his eyes were so dark, the irises appeared almost black, and he had the most sensuous mouth—full lips and flawless white teeth. Dear Lord Almighty, what a smile! A couple of days' worth of scruff made him appear even sexier and Megan clenched her hands together behind her back to keep from reaching out to run her fingers over his jaw. She was speechless, something that never happened to her. Not ever. Megan Mackenzie always, always had a quip or reply.

"Here." He offered the handkerchief again. "Please tell me those sad tears aren't for my pal Sean Flaherty." One black brow rose in a question. "I just ran into his brothers downstairs and they said he was going to be okay."

Megan accepted the handkerchief, passed it over her wet cheeks, and then blew her nose in as ladylike a manner as she could manage. "He *is* fine. I'm just... tired, I guess, and it's hard to see him all bandaged up. The nurse is with him right now."

"I don't believe we've met." The guy's smile nearly set Megan back on her heels. "I'm Vin DeLuca... and you are…?"

"*You're* Vinnie da Cop?" Megan couldn't believe this gorgeous creature was the Chicago police detective Sean had mentioned was his poker buddy for the last few years. He'd always referred to him as *Vinnie da Cop*, which he sorta said out of the side of his mouth, and had made Megan picture a middle-aged, rather round, and balding fellow. Sean had never once included the fact that the man was a dang Roman god.

Vin threw back his head and laughed—a sound that sent a shot of heat straight through her. "I am. My reputation precedes me apparently."

"I-I…" Heat suffused her face. Men did not affect her like this—she was the mayor of a town for pity's sake, not some high-school freshman. She refolded the handkerchief, taking a second to regroup. "I'll wash this and get it back to you."

"No need." Another killer grin. "I have dozens. My *nonna* sends me some every Christmas." He crossed his arms over his broad chest, his black eyes flashed, and *were those dimples creasing his cheeks?* "You know, I've been buddies with Sean Flaherty for at least eight years, and the last thing I expected to see this morning was an angel from heaven weeping outside his hospital room. So tell me, angel, who are you and why haven't I met you before now?"

Chapter Three

MEGAN WAS SAVED from further embarrassing herself by the arrival of Conor, Brendan, and Aidan, who surrounded the two of them, firing a barrage of questions about Sean. Meg stopped them from storming the hospital room and led the way to a small family waiting room at the end of the hall. "The nurse is with him right now," she said, gratefully accepting the cardboard container of coffee that Bren handed her.

"You've met Megs then?" Conor asked Vin as they all settled around a table that had a half-finished jigsaw puzzle on it. Of all the brothers, Conor had the most pronounced Irish lilt—something they'd all gotten from living with their parents, Irish immigrants Maggie and Donal Flaherty. The brogues really only manifested when they were stressed or deliberately trying to charm. Meg had heard the stressed version from all three of them last night.

"I was working on it when you guys crashed in." Vin turned his bone-melting smile on Megan.

It was an effort not to swoon, but she managed to get her act together enough to return the smile as Aidan made introductions.

"Megan Mackenzie, meet Vinnie da Cop. Vinnie, meet Megs da Mayor." Aidan grinned.

"*You're* the mayor of River's Edge?" Vin eyed her with even more interest, which sent Megan's heart racing. "Seems like I remember Sean saying something about being best friends with the mayor of his hometown. He failed to mention said mayor was a beautiful lady."

Brendan waved an open hand in front of Vin's face. "Turn down the charm, dude. Our Megs is a sweet sensible woman who eats womanizers like you for breakfast."

"I should be so lucky," Vin murmured, shoving Bren's hand away and giving Megan another dose of that smile. "Speaking of breakfast"—his black brow furrowed as he completely ignored the hoots of the Flaherty brothers— "would you like to join me in the café downstairs after I check in on Sean?"

Conor touched her arm and winked. "Meggy, me darlin', I'd be cautious with this one. He's got a line of broken hearts behind him longer than the Dan Ryan Expressway."

Brendan nodded, elbowing Vin in the ribs good-naturedly. "Con's right, ya know. Don't be listening to any of his blather. The man's a rake, I tell ya, a lecher."

Megan glanced around the table—all three brothers were grinning and their matching blue eyes twinkled. But when her eyes met Vin's again, the look in them was so sensual it nearly took her breath away. Who cared if this guy *was* a

Lothario? It was just breakfast. An hour sitting across the table from a guy so hot he made her spine liquefy sounded just fine to her. "I'd love breakfast, Vin." Childishly, she stuck her tongue out at Conor, who just shook his head sadly. "I'll go to the powder room and freshen up while you visit Sean."

Vin grinned triumphantly at the Flahertys and got up from the table. "I'll meet you outside his room." He strutted—there was no other word for it—out the door, heading back down the hall to Sean's room.

Megan couldn't help it. She watched that tight butt encased in jeans that fit perfectly—not too snug, not too loose—until Vin disappeared before she turned on Conor. "You think I can't handle a player, Con?"

"Here's the thing"—Conor folded his arms across his chest—"this guy's not just a player, he's the mac daddy of all players."

"The *what*?" Megan scowled. "What are you talking about?"

"He'll break your heart, sister," Bren supplied, shaking his too-long brown hair out of his eyes.

"Do you think that worries me? I've dated guys like him before." Megan knew when a guy was flirting with her—Vin DeLuca had definitely been flirting and doing it rather brilliantly at seven in the morning with a rumpled woman who had only slept for a couple of hours in the last day and a half. She had to confess she was enjoying it.

Brendan shook his head. "Not like Vinnie. He's a great guy who loves his grandma, goes to mass every Wednesday and Sunday, is a big brother to a fatherless inner-city kid, works one day a month at his church's soup kitchen, and has won a shelf full of awards from the Chicago PD. He sounds perfect, but he's a heartbreaker. Ask Sean, he'll tell you."

Aidan held up one finger. "He has women falling all over him constantly. Con loves to razz him about broken hearts, but Vinnie always tells the story differently. He'll tell you *he's* the one who gets his heart broken. Regularly." He gave her an arch look. "He also has a weakness for um… shall we say, buxom blondes."

Megan couldn't help it, she laughed out loud. "Buxom blondes? Aidan, seriously?" She mussed his perfect blond hair as she rose and passed behind him.

"Save yourself the pain, Megs." Conor shook his head, a pseudo-sad expression on his handsome face. "He's going to make you fall in love with him and then break your heart, but he'll claim all along it was his heart that got broken."

Brendan nodded. "Yup, and Sean'll have another six months of listening to Vinnie bemoan the fact that another woman has crushed him, when actually he did the crushing. We'd hate to see that happen to you."

Megan gazed at them, going from face to face, but they all managed to look perfectly serious. "Guys, it's breakfast. I'm pretty sure nobody's heart's going to get broken over hospital coffee and a stale doughnut." She stopped in the doorway to toss a saucy smile their way. "Besides, after all the crappy dates I've suffered through lately, a little spit-game with a gorgeous cop sounds pretty darn appealing."

SEAN HEAVED A sigh of relief when Colt finally signed off the computer and gave him a smart salute. "I'll be back in to check on you, my friend, but if you need anything at all, you just hit the call button. I'll come running." He spun around and marched out of the room, passing Vinnie DeLuca on his way in door.

"Hey, man." Vin's voice was low as he approached the bed, grinning. "Flaherty, you are messed up."

"Thanks for the update, Vin." Sean dropped his head back tiredly. All he really wanted was to go back to sleep.

"Are you in a lot of pain?" Vin stood by the bedside, his eyes darting from Sean to the machinery surrounding him, clearly fascinated by all the monitors and tubing and pulleys. "They ought to be keeping you pretty well dosed up."

Sean shook his head and sighed. "Just so freakin' uncomfortable and confused and—" He caught his breath and panic set in as everything hit him like a bolt of lightning. He'd been shot! Shot on the steps of the Evanston courthouse with... *oh, dear Lord!* He struggled to sit up. "Vin! Where's Kent?" His mind raced as memories flooded his brain. "Was anyone else hit? Did they get her?" A monitor started beeping and he grabbed the hand Vin was resting on the safety bar. "She wanted me dead, Vin! She went batshit and she wanted me dead. God... oh, God..." He couldn't breathe. His heart was pounding out of his chest and he tried again to pull himself up, but the damn traction kept him prisoner.

"Hey, hey. Calm down now." Vin's eyes widened as he watched the heart rate monitor and gently pressed Sean back against the pillows. "You're okay, buddy. Kent's okay. He didn't get hit. Nobody else got hurt." Vin spoke in a low singsong voice while he held one hand on Sean's chest. "Easy now, easy."

"I gotta get to Kent," Sean insisted, the fear building. "She's going to kill him."

"No, she's not. She's in custody."

"Are you sure? Are you certain they got her?" The scene kept replaying in his head, the press congregating around him and Kent, the report of Kent's crazy ex, Missy's pistol, her irrational threats, the cries of the crowd... Sobs welled up in his chest and he tried to swallow them, but they burst out in a choked groan that shocked even him in its intensity. Vinnie's eyes got bigger still and even though his lips were moving, his words faded in the jumble of horror that overtook Sean.

Suddenly his hospital room filled with people—his brothers, the damn chipper nurse, and when he blinked and took his eyes off Vinnie, there was Megan standing at the end of his bed.

"Sean." Her serene tone seemed to come from miles away as she placed her hands on his left foot. "Sean, look at me."

He trembled violently as he tried to focus on her in spite of his brothers crowding around Vin, and the nurse messing with the drawer next to his bed. God, he couldn't breathe. His breath was stuck in his throat and he was dizzy. Colt produced a white paper bag and instructed him to breathe into it. Megan kept her gaze pinned to his while she rubbed his ankle, then his calf with both hands.

"Sean. Breathe now." Hers was the only voice he could sort out of the babble that filled the small space. "Just breathe."

He kept his eyes on her, watching her encouraging smile as she stroked from his knee to his ankle to his toes, murmuring the whole time. Colt said something unintelligible and brought Megan around to the right side of the bed to put her hand on Sean's. It hurt his shoulder to move it but no way was he going to let loose of her fingers. She was safety, reality, his best friend… she was *home*.

His brothers' low voices were background noise as his breath came easier and his heart slowed just a little. He lowered the paper bag.

Colt, who now hovered above him on the other side of the bed, stared at the heart monitor. "Steady now. Pulse is slowing. You gonna be okay?"

Sean closed his eyes, but kept his grip on Megan's hand, and nodded wordlessly. He *was* going to be okay, but the replay of the shooting that continued to loop in his head still sent an occasional shudder through him.

When he opened his eyes, there was Conor next to Meg, his blue eyes nearly navy with concern holding the glass with the bendy straw. "Try a sip of water, Sean."

"That's a good idea," Colt agreed, ever watchful as he typed into the bedside computer. "I can get you something to help you calm down if you want. Doc has an order in for Ativan PRN."

Sean *didn't* want that. He wanted to be clear, to hear the whole story of what happened, to talk to Kent, and most of all, to keep Meg's warm fingers interlaced with his own. "No, thanks." He swallowed some water. "I'm good now."

Colt raised one brow. "Sure?"

"Yeah." Sean attempted a smile, which probably looked more like a grimace as another flash of terror arced through him. But he wanted Colt gone so he could talk to his brothers and Vinnie. He needed details.

"Okey doke." Colt checked the IV line one more time. "Your breakfast, such as it is, should be here shortly. Eat it and you'll advance to real food a lot faster." He gave the rest of the room a hard stare over the top of his glasses. "Don't tire him out and hit that call button if you see any signs of stress again, okay? I'll check back in a few."

Sean really did smile then as all three of his brothers

nodded vigorously like little boys who'd just been scolded.

Megan released his hand, leaving him somewhat bereft, but when she stepped back, Conor, Bren, and Aidan lined up beside the bed. Vinnie went around to the other side, tossing Meg a noticeably intimate smile as he brushed past her at the foot of the bed. She blushed and suddenly became very busy straightening the blankets over Sean's foot.

What was *that* about?

"You scared the crap out of us, bro." Aidan spoke up first, the big grin on his face belying the fear showing in his eyes. "Stopping a bullet with your body is not something you do in real life. You want to do that again, come out to the coast and I'll get you a guest spot on *LA Detectives*."

As they all chuckled, Sean looked from Flaherty to Flaherty to Flaherty—each face was etched with worry and fear, and he was struck by how much Bren and Conor looked like Da, while Aidan resembled their mother with his blond hair and smaller build, but they all four had Da's blue eyes. His throat tightened. His brothers had dropped everything to fly to his side, and even though he would've done exactly the same thing had it been one of them, it still touched him deeply. Living alone in Chicago, he sometimes forgot how much it meant to him to belong to a large, loving family.

"Someone should call Char and let her know I'm okay." His voice still trembled, so he took in another deep breath of hospital air. Their stepmother would be worried senseless.

"We called her last night after your surgery." Conor put

an arm around Brendan's shoulders. "She sends her love. So do Sam and Ali. I've been fielding texts all night from everyone down home. They're all worried sick about you and impressed as hell that you made the national news."

"I-I what?" Conor's words weren't registering. *The national news?*

"Yup." Brendan grinned. "CNN picked up the story from WGN—*Chicago attorney saves client's life.*"

"You're a hero, man," Vinnie added, giving him a light fist to his good shoulder.

Sean shook his head. "That's not what happened." He was no hero. He'd simply jerked Kent down after he'd realized Missy was shooting. It was instinct. "You're sure Kent's okay?"

"He's fine, I promise," Vin said and the brothers all nodded in agreement. "He's telling everyone you saved his life, shielded his body with yours. That sounds pretty heroic to me, dude."

Sean sighed. "It was instinct. Pure instinct." His head was throbbing again and he was feeling just a touch nauseated. Probably needed to eat, although it didn't sound like he was going to get much today.

"Oh come on, big boy, be the hero." Meg tapped his foot. "It's your fifteen minutes of fame—go for it." Her smile warmed him down to his toes and for the first time since he woke up, he really felt like smiling. God, it was so good to see her, to have her here. Meg always made everything better, even traction seemed less dire with her in the room. How like her to simply get in her car and head north when she heard the news—definitely the sign of a true friend.

"*The Tribune* wants an interview. There's a cute little reporter downstairs, sucking down coffee and waiting to talk to you." Aidan waggled his eyebrows, then winked.

"I'm gonna say no on Sean's behalf. He needs rest." Brendan bumped Aidan's shoulder with his own. "Why don't you guys go back to the hotel suite? I'll take first watch here." He backed away from the bed and settled into the recliner Meg had occupied earlier.

"No, no. Don't do a hotel. Stay at my place. Con, find my keys—they should be here, shouldn't they?" Sean glanced around, once again catching something—a look—between Vin and Megan that left him feeling perturbed and a little anxious, although he couldn't imagine why. "It's only a couple of miles from here. You can Uber. The app's on my phone—wherever that is."

"We've got it covered, big brother, at least for a couple of nights." Conor patted Sean's head affectionately, unaware that mere touch set off another throb of pain in Sean's skull. "And Bren's got your stuff, so no worries."

He managed a feeble wave as Conor and Aidan trooped out of the room, then closed his eyes.

"You look exhausted." Megan came around by Vinnie to press her lips to Sean's forehead. "Get some rest, buddy. I'll be back up this afternoon, okay?"

He opened his eyes. "Where are you going?" He tried not to sound like a whiny child, but the proprietary way Vin had his hand on her back bugged him.

"I've got a room at the same hotel as the guys." Megan stroked his hair off his forehead and somehow *her* touch was soothing rather than painful. "I'm going to go get a shower and change."

"But first, I'm taking her to breakfast. The woman needs sustenance and I'm just the guy to provide it." Vinnie swung his shoulders in a fake cocky gesture that Sean usually found funny.

It wasn't funny today.

Chapter Four

"I'VE NEVER HAD breakfast with a mayor before." Vin set their plates and cups in front of them and put the empty tray on the table behind him. Somehow, he'd had managed to score a quiet corner table in the crowded, noisy hospital cafeteria, which both pleased and concerned Megan. It was nice to be away from the bustle, but alone with Vin, she'd have to be at least somewhat entertaining. He was delicious, but she simply wasn't sure she had it in her.

"Well this mayor is beat, so she won't expect you to bow or genuflect." Megan hung her purse on the back of her chair before dropping into it. She wanted to be perky, she really did; but exhaustion overtook her and she could barely manage a smile. She stared at the fluffy pile of scrambled eggs, wondering if she had the strength to lift a fork, even a plastic one.

"You poor thing." Vin's gorgeous black eyes were full of compassion. "You've got to be dead on your feet." He unwrapped her utensils and set them on a napkin beside her plate. "Come on, you need some food. Eat, then I'll walk you to your hotel."

As Vin watched, Meg removed the lid from her coffee cup and let the scent of steaming brew fill her nostrils. Strengthened only a little, she added cream and a packet of sugar, stirred, and sipped. After a couple more swallows, she felt almost human again. She offered him a halfhearted smile.

"There's what I've been looking for." He grinned and once again, Megan was struck by how incredibly good-looking he was. Tierney and Sam would be drooling. "You're the youngest mayor I've ever met. How'd that happen?"

Meg smiled. She'd told this story plenty of times before and her eggs were cooling, so she kept it brief. "I was voted onto the town council a few years ago. They were looking for fresh meat, I think, and I'd always been interested in making River's Edge better." She sipped some more coffee, closing her eyes in appreciation before she continued. "The mayor at the time had been mayor forever and he just sorta ran the town like his own little fiefdom. So next time he came up for election, I tossed my hat into the ring and I won. That was four years ago."

Vin munched on a slice of bacon. "Was the old mayor pissed?"

She shrugged. "Oh, probably a little, but he got over it. The town threw him a huge bon voyage when he moved to Arizona not long after he lost the election. I still get Christmas cards from him. And now my town's moving into the twenty-first century and most everyone's onboard, so it's been good."

"The guys tell me you drove up here as soon as you heard. Left your official duties to be at Sean's side." He tilted his head and raised his chin a notch. "You two must be really tight."

Megan nodded as she tucked into the eggs, which were surprisingly tasty. "Since fifth grade." She spread jam on her English muffin. "We've been buddies forever."

"Always *just* buddies?" Vin was suddenly fascinated with his own breakfast, not meeting her gaze.

His question sent an electric charge through her in spite of how tired she was, and she wondered if what the Flahertys had told her about Vinnie da Cop could actually be true—that he was attracted to her. An intriguing notion. It had been way too long since she'd been this drawn to a man at first sight. Tierney would accuse her of being shallow because, okay, this initial attraction *was* purely physical, but what was wrong with that really? Besides, he was also kind and the fact that he hung out with Sean scored him more points. Most important, he seemed to be fascinated by her and after all the horrible dates she'd had lately, she couldn't help wanting to bask in his attention for just a short time.

However, Conor's words sent up a tiny red flag—did Vinnie really fall in love in a New York, well, a *Chicago* minute and then become a heartbreaker? She snuck a peek at him, his dark hair falling over his forehead, his full lips curved in a half-smile as he smeared apple butter on a biscuit, then popped the whole thing in his mouth. She tried to remember the last time a man had fallen head over heels for her. Probably Bobby Jensen in seventh grade… and Sean had threatened the poor kid with being a permanent soprano when he wouldn't stop following Megan around town. Pretty much, Sean had always had her back when it came to guys and dates, offering his opinion, sometimes setting her up with his buddies on the basketball team, always being a shoulder to cry on when things went south. Maybe she should talk to him about this delectable police detective.

Vin gave her a curious look and she realized she'd gotten so lost in her own thoughts, she hadn't answered his question.

Heat rose to her cheeks. "I'm sorry, Vin, I was… drifting, I guess."

"Lack of sleep will do that to you." Vin shot her the dimples and her belly contracted. He gazed at her earnestly. "So, just buddies then? You and Sean?" He gave a little self-conscious shrug. "I want to ask you to dinner tonight, but I don't want to piss off Flaherty, not when he's got all three brothers here for backup."

"You don't even know me," Megan dissembled as she mentally tossed her suitcase for something appropriate to wear to a nice restaurant.

"I *want* to know you."

"I don't have anything to wear." Megan didn't know why she was messing with him when she fully intended to accept his invitation. Sean would likely get a huge kick out of her having a date with Vinnie da Cop. And in spite of what the other Flaherty brothers had told her, she figured Vin's heart was safe since she wasn't going to be in Chicago more than a few days, and the last time *she'd* fallen in love, it had taken much longer than that.

"SEE?" VINNIE WAVED one hand expressively as if to encompass all of Quartino Ristorante. "You're perfect." His dark eyes swept over her in an appreciative and intimate gaze.

He was right—in her jeans, white V-neck shirt, scarf, and long red cardigan, she fit right in at the rustic yet elegant restaurant they had walked to from the hotel. Vin, handsome in jeans, a black T-shirt, and a camel-colored sport coat, turned the head of nearly every woman they passed. Megan couldn't deny a little thrill at being on the arm of a guy other women were salivating over, so she didn't object when he reached for her hand and linked his fingers with hers.

Quartino filled two light and airy floors with wooden tables, each one holding a stack of plates—intriguing. When the hostess led them past the bar, Megan couldn't help her quick intake of breath at the gorgeous carved wood, mirrors, and tall glass shelves filled with every imaginable kind of liquor.

She inhaled as they sat at a cozy table in a corner just past the bar area. The air was redolent with delicious aromas—garlic, roasting meat, pepperoni—and was she actually smelling red wine? "Why do all the tables have plates stacked on them?" She accepted a menu from the hostess. "Is this like an Italian tapas bar?"

Vin's grin sent a tingle down her spine. "That's exactly what it is." He opened his menu. "They do small plates so we can taste as many things as you want."

Their server appeared—a compact, handsome man with gray-streaked dark hair, who looked to be any age from forty to sixty—and slapped Vin on the shoulder. "Vincenzo!" He set his water pitcher on the table.

"Stefano!" Vin jumped to his feet and the two men greeted each other with exuberant bro-hugs.

The man turned to Megan. "And who is this lovely lady?"

"Meet Megan Mackenzie, the mayor of River's Edge, Indiana." Vin settled back into his chair while Stefano pressed a mustachioed kiss on Megan's hand. "Megan, my buddy, Stefano Nibali. He's no relation to the Italian cyclist, so don't believe him when he tells you he can get you an autograph."

"Madam Mayor, we're honored to have you with us." He eyed her with the same intimate, appreciative look she'd gotten from Vin earlier. "And I do confess to sometimes using the Nibali name to my own advantage, but how else can a simple server impress beautiful, successful ladies like yourself?"

Heat rose to her face. *Dear Lord, blushing again? Seriously?* Sam would laugh her butt off.

"It's nice to meet you." She recovered quickly and offered him a smile. "I'm a huge Tour de France fan, so *I* confess to being a little disappointed you're not Nibali's cousin. He's a particular favorite of mine. I was heartsick when he crashed out last summer."

Stefano nodded. "As we all were. Sorry I can't introduce you to him. Can I make it up to you with a basket of bread and a bottle of Chianti while you look over the menu?" He picked up the water pitcher and filled two glasses.

"Bread and wine make everything better," Megan agreed, mentally cursing the heat still burning her cheeks.

Stefano turned to Vin, his expression full of concern. "How is Sean? We've all been worried sick."

"I saw him earlier today. He's going to be okay." Vin lifted his chin toward Megan. "Megan is actually here for him. They've been friends since they were kids. His brothers are with him this evening, so I stole her away."

Stefano's dark brows came together in a V and he slapped his forehead. "Of course! River's Edge. Sean's hometown."

Meg smiled up at the server. "You know Sean? Is he a regular here?"

"He's been coming here since we opened over ten years ago." Stefano tipped his head in Vin's direction. "He and this guy turn up at least once a week for small plates and Chianti. Let me get you that bread and wine while you peruse the menu."

Megan smiled as Stefano hurried off, but when she turned back to Vin, the slightly bedazzled expression on his handsome face set her back. It was not how men usually looked at her, and the look in his dark eyes warmed her to her toes. Heat rose in her cheeks again, so she busied herself with the menu, which looked wonderful.

"Promise me you won't order just a salad?" Vin's voice was deep and smoky.

"What if that's all I want?" For reasons completely unknown to her, this guy brought out the flirt in her.

Oh, that's a lie. The reason is he's hot and he clearly thinks you are, too.

Disappointment shuttered his face for the briefest second. "Well, I guess that's what you should get, but if you do, you'll miss the salumeria tasting I was going to recommend"—he pointed to the top of the menu—"which includes such an amazing array of meats and cheeses and salads and olives that you'll want to fling yourself into my arms with joy." He raised one dark brow and offered her a wistful smile.

Megan gazed at him. She already wanted to throw herself into his arms and she was pretty sure he was completely aware of that fact because every time he touched her, she shivered. Plus, the salumeria sounded delicious, and she was starving. "Can it include the roasted beet salad?"

He chuckled, tossed the menu aside with a satisfied smile, and reached for her hand. "It includes any salad your heart desires, *bellissimo*."

Megan settled back into her chair and breathed, truly breathed, for the first time in forty-eight hours. Sean was going to be okay, he was safe in the hospital, his brothers were with him, and Vin's warm fingers around hers banished the last of her defenses.

When Sean opened his eyes, the room was dim and the curtains had been pulled across the windows. For a second, he tensed, absorbing the scent of hospital air, the quiet in the hallway outside his half-closed door, and the incessant beeping of one of the damn monitors above his head. That must've been what woke him from the dream he'd been having, which was already fading from his head. He and Megs had been riding bikes along the Ohio River, but they were both younger, like junior-high age, and she had her blond hair in the long braid she'd always worn—the one that swung over her shoulder when she turned her head toward him. He closed his eyes, trying desperately to return to the bike path at home and the ring of Meg's clear laughter, but the monitor was insistent.

He fumbled by his pillow for the remote when Conor

stepped up to the bed. "Here, let me get that for you."

Conor pulled the remote up from where it hung over the side of the bed and touched the call button. He wandered around to the other side and peered at the beeping monitor, his gaze following the IV line that was threaded through it to the bag hanging on a hook. "Looks like your IV is empty." He hit a button on the machine and mercifully, shut off the annoying noise. "Someone should be here shortly."

"What time is it?"

"About midnight." Conor smoothed the hair off Sean's forehead soothing the anxiety building inside him somewhat. "You should try to go back to sleep."

"That's all I've been doing." Sean licked his lips. His mouth was dry and tasted like the entire Russian army had marched through it in dirty socks.

"You want some water?" Conor poured from an ice-and-water-filled pitcher and handed him the glass with the straw.

Sean drank deeply. "I want a steak." He managed a feeble grin, hoping to erase some of the worry etched on his brother's face. "What are you doing here at midnight?"

Conor returned the smile. "My shift. Are you in pain?"

"A little. Not bad. My mind is so... fuzzy." Sean rubbed his jaw, startled at the amount of stubble there. "And not just my brain apparently. God, how long have I been here?"

"You're officially going into day three. The fuzziness is the pain meds. You've been on some bodacious stuff, dude, but they're starting to draw it down." With a grin, Conor settled into the big recliner by the bed. "Welcome back. The doc says the traction comes off today and you'll get to stand up, maybe try a few steps. We gotta get you out of this bed."

Sean was almost afraid to ask. "When can I get out of here?"

"You probably have another day or so in the hospital and then you're going to a rehab on the other side of the hospital for a week or ten days, depending on how well you do with physical therapy."

"After that?" The vagueness was starting to clear and for the first time since he'd been shot, Sean was becoming alert. He had so many questions, still a few about the shooting, but mostly ones about what was going to happen to him.

Conor leaned forward in the chair. "We're bringing you home after rehab."

"Home?"

"Home to River's Edge."

"But... but my cases. I can't leave Chicago. I have to go back to work... and..." Panic welled up inside his chest, making breathing difficult and Conor jumped up to lay a hand on Sean's chest.

"Hey, breathe." He leaned in. "Look at me, Sean."

Sean met his brother's dark blue eyes and the anxiety subsided somewhat as he stared at him.

Conor rubbed a circle on his chest, then patted him, his gaze never wavering. "Take it easy. Everything's under control."

"Is it?" Sean grabbed Conor's hand and clung to it. "I gotta work and I can't freaking walk. My right arm is in a sling and—"

"Right now, your job is to heal." Conor squeezed his hand, but didn't let go. "Charlie Smith was here earlier. Well, yesterday, do you remember that?"

He did have a nebulous recollection of Charlie's big laugh and booming voice. "I do, but I can't remember everything he said."

"You're going on sabbatical for a few months. Your cases are covered and your office will be there when you get back. Your health insurance is amazing. You'll be on short-term disability, so you'll have 60 percent of your salary coming in, and Charlie says that will easily keep your rent and utilities paid up here while you're down home."

"Con, I *can't* go home. I'm too booked. I've got to get through rehab next week and get back to work." The panic intensified, but Sean was determined to breathe through it— no more paper bags. "Wait, did you say I'll be on disability?" *Disability!* That word scared the holy crap out of him.

His brother raised one dark brow. "I said *short-term* disability. Charlie says your policy allows up to fifty-two weeks but—"

"*A year!*" The only thing that kept Sean from leaping from the hospital bed was the fact that his right leg was hanging in the air, but that didn't stop him from lifting his entire torso from the mattress, which of course, sent a bolt of fire through his shoulder and another through his leg. He dropped back, exhausted from the effort and the emotionality.

"I didn't say you'd be off work for a year." Conor used the singsongy soothing voice that everyone had been using, the one that was really starting to annoy the hell out of Sean. "I said you have *up to a year*, but you'll be back on your feet long before then."

"Damn straight." The words came out weaker than he intended, but Sean was so fatigued, it was an effort to even form words.

"There's the Sean we know and love." Conor smiled, straightened the covers, and plumped the pillows. "Doc says you need time to heal and we decided you'll do that better down where you'll have people to help you. You'll stay at Char's because she's all on one floor. Nate and some of the boys from the high school are already building a ramp over her front steps to get you in the house and Char's doorways are easily big enough to accommodate a wheelchair. We ordered you this awesome ultralight electric model that—"

Sean's heart rose to his throat. "A wheelchair? What's wrong with crutches?"

"Your shoulder injury won't handle crutches or a walker yet, so you'll be tooling around in this way-cool candy-apple-red job that will support your cast. Just for a few weeks until your shoulder heals. Here, I'll show it to you." Conor dug his phone out of his pocket and began tapping the screen.

Although Sean knew in his head that his brothers were doing exactly what he would do if one of them was injured, it still pissed him off that they'd simply taken charge—ordering a wheelchair, building a ramp... Did Char even want him at her house? He closed his eyes while Conor googled. He'd spoken to Char on Aidan's phone. Was it yesterday or the day before? He didn't remember much of the conversation except she'd been a little weepy, but very happy he was okay. Had she said something about staying with her? That seemed familiar.

Suddenly the logistics of getting down to River's Edge, staying with his stepmother in the house he'd grown up in, learning to use a wheelchair, doing rehab... God, how would he even use the bathroom or shower? "Con, how can... how will I..." He couldn't form the myriad questions that filled his head and his voice was croaky with fear. Tears burned behind his eyelids. Dammit, how he hated feeling so helpless.

Conor glanced up, then dropped his phone back in his pocket and gripped Sean's hand. "We've got you, brother. You're good. Meg's already hired a nurse to come in and he can help you do everything you need to do at home. Mary Louise Shafer even offered us the use of her wheelchair-accessible van. It's just been sitting in her garage since Mike died. She's been thinking about selling it, but she's happy for us to use it until you can get out of the chair. It's time to come home and heal, Sean."

"But…" A lump formed in Sean's throat and he swallowed hard as tears leaked out and ran down his cheeks. *Crying?* He hadn't cried since Da's funeral, not since the night he and his brothers had sat on barrels in the wine cellar and toasted their father with his prize chambourcin. When he met Conor's eyes, tears glistened in their blue depths, too.

Conor handed him a tissue. "These things cost twenty bucks apiece, so let's keep the waterworks to a minimum, okay?"

Sean laughed in spite of his tears. "I've got great insurance, remember?"

Conor pressed a kiss to the top of his head. "It's all going to be okay, big brother. I promise."

Chapter Five

"HEY, CHECK ME out, Megs!" Taking a deep breath, Sean lifted his right arm and showed off his bicep, then he raised it above his head and clasped his hands together in a boxer's traditional gesture of triumph.

Megan's lips curved up in a big smile. "You are killing it, dude!" She glanced over at Ollie, the male nurse who'd been his constant companion since he'd arrived in River's Edge four weeks ago. "He's doing so amazing, isn't he?"

Oliver Garcia just nodded from his chair next to the PT table in St. Mark's Emergency and Health Services. "I'm gonna be out of a gig pretty soon, and, *dios mío*, I am going to hate leaving Miss Char's home cooking."

His Latino heritage showed not only in his soft accent, but also in his stocky, muscular frame, black hair, and dark eyes. He might have been nearly a head shorter, but he'd been hauling Sean's bulk around as easily as if Sean had been a child.

"This guy isn't going to need me anymore once that cast comes off."

Sean rubbed his aching shoulder before doing a few more

reps with the right arm. "I'm going to miss you, man, but it will be nice to be able to take a leak all by myself." He was kidding about the privacy—he'd mastered *that* the first day he was home, but he sure wasn't joking about missing his nurse. Ollie was the best.

The brawny nurse had been waiting at the airport in Louisville along with Conor, Sam, Ali, Bren, and Char when the plane landed. After joyful but tearful hellos from his family, it had been Ollie who'd shown him how to manipulate the new red electric wheelchair. He'd patiently demonstrated all the features and made Sean practice right there in the airport parking lot before he lowered the lift on Mike Shafer's van and said, "Okay, *hombre*, the lift switch is by the door. Get yourself in there."

Sean's heart had dropped that day when Ollie put one hand on Megan's shoulder to keep her from helping him into the borrowed van. Tired and defeated, he only wanted to go home to Char's and take a nap, but the energetic nurse had just cocked his head toward the van. "Get going and don't forget to lock your chair into the lift or you'll slide out the back and they'll be picking pieces of you and that fancy-ass chair off the road for days."

The moment had pretty much set the stage for the Sean-and-Ollie show. From that day forward, Oliver Garcia had been Sean's relentless advocate, but his first question in any situation was always, eternally, *so whatcha gonna do here, hombre?*

NAN REINHARDT

Sean knew how hard it must be on his family and friends to watch him tussle one-handed with dressing and eating and damn near everything else he had to do, because he'd feel the same if one of his brothers was in his position. He'd seen Char itch to cut his meat and help him shift from the wheelchair to the sofa or recliner. He'd caught her making his bed one day and had to remind her it was *his* job and that Ollie would kick both their butts if he saw her smoothing his bedspread or fluffing his pillows. Conor and Sam struggled with the urge to do things for him, too, clearing his dishes away when they stopped by to share a meal or grabbing a book or his laptop when it was just out of reach, unless Ollie caught them and gave them the stink-eye.

At first, Sean had resented the hell out of the nurse for stopping anyone who stepped in to help, but when his sensible brain took over, he knew Ollie was right. He'd never heal and get strong again if everyone coddled him. Even the therapist he'd been talking to once a week since he'd gotten home had agreed, telling him that the PTSD would grab him when he least expected it. Confidence and feeling strong physically were the best way to fight the darkness that sometimes shadowed his thoughts. And the gloom did sneak in, mostly at night when sleep eluded him and he was unable to get comfortable on the big bed in Char's guest room—the room he'd shared with Brendan growing up.

Those nights, he turned his focus to happy thoughts, like helping Conor in the vineyards when he was out of the

54

damn wheelchair. Buds were breaking and it was time for the spring work of maintaining the wires and poles that supported the vines. Conor came by most evenings after closing the winery to fill him in on the progress of the vines and talk about such things as pest mitigation and chemical versus natural control. Sean had been fascinated and had begun reading viticulture websites on his iPad in the evenings, as well as books from Da's library. Beat the hell out of television and at least he could converse with more knowledge when Conor visited. Soon he'd be on his feet again and he could join his brother in the vineyard.

Bren called every other day just to chat and Aidan picked up the opposite days, so he was in contact with at least two of his brothers each day. A couple of times Sam had come to him for advice with a knotty legal question, and Harry stopped in now and again with town news and campaign updates. The race for circuit court judge between the dapper attorney and the sitting judge was heating up, and Sean offered to make calls for him when the docs released him from the wheelchair. Charlie Smith and other attorneys from the firm checked in once a week, catching him up on what was happening in Chicago.

Megan was ever-present, popping into Char's at lunchtime with something yummy from the diner or meeting him and Ollie for a stroll in the shade of the redbuds along the River Walk or taking him into town after PT for pie and a glass of iced tea.

And then there was Vinnie, who texted at least twice a day with funny cop stories or reports on who was in his chair at the weekly poker game or pictures of Lake Michigan gleaming in the early summer sun. Sean laughed out loud at one shot that included a group of lovely young women on the beach with the caption, *they're waiting for you, dude.*

He was aware Vin was texting Megan as well—a thought that bugged him, although he couldn't say why, because it was *he* and Megs who spent time together nearly every day. Here in River's Edge, they were back to their old teasing friendship, talking about everything under the sun on the evenings she didn't have meetings or town business. They wandered the River Walk together, with her matching her stride to the pace of his electric wheelchair.

She was his most ardent cheerleader as well as great company—something he'd forgotten during his busy life in Chicago. Her wry sense of humor and intelligence had entertained him for years, but had she always been so adorable? And if so, how had he missed that fact in all the years they'd been friends?

Meg was also the only one who never tried to sneak help past Ollie. She cheered him on and brought him treats from the diner or the ice cream parlor or Paula's Bread and Butter Bakery, but never once attempted to assist him in any way. She was as steadfast as ever—his buddy, right by his side just as she'd promised she would be, but she was as fierce as Ollie and the physical therapist about him doing things for himself.

Megan interrupted his musing by tossing him a towel from the stack by the PT table. "Dude, you about done here? We're meeting Sam at Dad's for pie."

"A few more reps." Sean inhaled a deep breath, counting ten more arm raises as he released it.

Meg's phone chimed, and the goofy grin he'd come to begrudge crossed her face as she saw who had texted her. Sean grabbed the towel she'd tossed at him, wiped beads of sweat from his brow, then wrapped the towel around his neck, trying hard not to watch as Megan thumbed a reply.

Time to get dressed and get out of here. He shoved himself up from the table too fast and tipped sideways. Ollie leaped up and caught him before he went down on the floor. Heat scorched Sean's cheeks when Megan glanced up from her phone, then dropped it into the small purse hanging over her shoulder.

She trotted over to grasp his right bicep gingerly and help Ollie settle him into his red wheelchair before she exploded. "Cripes. Sean, watch it! You're doing great, but don't get all crazy on us." It was the first time, she'd ever helped him and as she let her hand slide down his arm, the touch sent an odd quivery sensation through him.

What the hell? He was getting goofy being confined to this damn chair if his old pal's touch was making him tingle like a fifteen-year-old. He shook his head at his own foolishness and a snort of laughter escaped. This was Meg, for

Pete's sake.

She jerked her hand away, completely misinterpreting the sound. "What? Did I hurt you?" She came around to the front of the chair to peer anxiously into his face. "Oh, Sean, I'm sorry!"

"You didn't hurt me." The words came out brusquer than he meant for them to, so he gave her a grin and a wink. "I'm feeling so strong, I keep forgetting I can't just stand up and move when I want to." He met Ollie's knowing gaze over her blond head.

His nurse didn't miss a trick. No doubt once they hit the locker room, Sean was in for another discourse from Ollie on how he should examine his feelings for Megan. Ollie was convinced Sean was jealous of Vin and Megan's growing relationship. Dude was being ridiculous, of course. He and Megs were, and always had been, just friends, but Ollie wasn't buying it. Friends can become lovers, he'd told Sean just the other night and Sean had scoffed. Impossible! Not he and Megs. Never he and Megs.

But the seed had been planted and now, as he saw the concern in her brandy-colored eyes, felt the brush of her curls against his cheek, his breath hitched and he wondered what it would be like to kiss her the way he'd seen Vin kiss her when she'd gotten into Sam's car at the airport the day they left Chicago.

MEGAN COULDN'T HELP the sigh of pure pleasure that escaped as she tasted the first bite of key lime pie. Too bad for Sam that an office emergency had kept her from joining them. When she glanced up at Sean, his expression showed just as much enjoyment. Nobody made pies like Paula Meadows, not even Dad and he was a gourmet chef. "Too bad Ollie's missing this."

"Yeah," Sean agreed after swallowing another forkful of creamy lime deliciousness. "He had some errands to run up on the highway." He took a sip of iced tea. "Two more weeks and I can drive again, Mary Louise gets her van back, and Ollie gets a new gig."

Megan loved his enthusiasm, but doubted his timeline. "Is that what the doctor says? Even if he removes the cast, are you sure you'll be driving right away?"

Sean gave her the over-the-top-of-the glasses look that had turned her on in junior high, annoyed the heck out of her in high school, and now just made her smile.

Since the shooting, he'd taken to wearing his glasses again instead of contacts. He looked good, even kind of sexy, a thought she'd shoved aside almost as soon as it popped into her head because that wasn't how she ever allowed herself to think of Sean.

"Okay, maybe not driving," he said, "but at least out of the wheelchair and using a cane or something."

"Yeah, but remember he's only checking it." Megan wiped her mouth with a paper napkin. "I don't want to be a downer here, but there's a chance he may put another one on if things aren't quite healed up yet. Be prepared for that."

"I *am* prepared for that." He furrowed his brow before excited light gleamed in his blue eyes. "Ollie says there's a chance I'll go to something removable so I can start working the knee. Plus I've read everything there is to read on this kind of injury. That's often the protocol."

She held up one hand. "Okay. I just don't want you to push too hard and reinjure your leg."

He grinned. "Are you afraid I'll end up in your hair way longer than a few months, or are you just anxious for me to get back to Chicago, so you'll have someplace to stay while you're visiting Vinnie?"

His playful tone reminded Megan of high school and all the times he'd teased her mercilessly about whomever she was dating. Some things never changed. Sean gave her endless crap about every guy she fell for and apparently life as big-city lawyer hadn't matured that out of him. "Why wouldn't I just stay with Vin?"

His eyes widened as he gasped in obvious fake shock. "Why, Megan Therese Mackenzie! Are you telling me that things with Vinnie have passed mere flirtation?"

"Why would I tell you anything, you nosy jerkwad?"

Sean leaned on the table, his chin in his palm. "Because we're besties?" he offered, fluttering his long dark lashes in a silly girly imitation. "Tell me everything. Did you two do the nasty while you were in Chicago?" He lowered his tone to a hushed whisper. "Are you guys having phone sex? C'mon, dish."

"Don't be an idiot, Sean." Heat burned in Megan's cheeks because his assumptions weren't that far off the mark. No, she hadn't slept with Vin while she was in Chicago, despite his delicious, persuasive kisses after the few short dates they'd had when she wasn't with Sean in the hospital. The physical attraction between she and Vin was undeniable—one of the big reasons she'd had never invited him back to her hotel room, and why she'd never seen his apartment in spite of his broad hints. She'd have had him flat on his back in the time it took him to kick off his shoes and that fact scared the crap out of her. Something in the clear-thinking part of her brain kept telling her to take it slow with Vinnie da Cop.

Maybe she was old-fashioned, but she never fell into bed with a guy after a couple of dates—especially not since she'd been elected mayor of River's Edge. A certain level of circumspection was required in her position and Meg respected those limits. It was a small town and people loved to talk. She'd never be able to move River's Edge into the future if the citizens were more interested in gossiping about their mayor than talking about progress. Besides, she and Vin lived several hundred miles apart. However, he hadn't let the distance between them stop him, and their phone conversations since she'd been home had become progressively more intimate.

Sean pointed one long finger at her. "Ah ha! You're blushing. I know he's texting you several times a day because you get this goofy smile on your face when you check your phone. Is he sexting? Has he sent you a picture of his junk yet?" The last question came out with such a sour expression that Megan leaned back, surprised at his tone. He wasn't joking around anymore.

Glancing around the mostly empty diner, she assured herself that their conversation was strictly between them. Then she folded her arms across her breasts and narrowed her eyes at him. "I cannot believe you asked me that, Sean Donal Flaherty. What are we? Still in junior high? My gosh, you must really need a date, dude, if *my* sex life is so damn enthralling."

He merely smirked, shrugged, and took another bite of pie. "I know him. It's a legitimate question."

"Well, I've got a *legitimate question* for you. What is your problem with me and Vin?" She shoved her pie aside and plopped her arms on the table in front of her, trying very hard to keep the indignation rising in her at bay.

They needed to have this conversation because even though Sean had been teasing her about Vin, it seemed lately the joking had become a little too snarky.

"I don't have a problem with you and Vin." He finished his pie and wiped his face. "I think you and Vinnie are cute as hell together."

Even as he said the words, she doubted their sincerity.

"Well, there's a ringing endorsement. Thanks for your support, pal."

Sean winced as he moved his shoulder and settled back against the red vinyl booth. She wondered if he was uncomfortable physically or just with the conversation. His gaze wandered around the diner, focused everywhere except on her. More weirdness. She and Sean didn't have awkward moments between them, but the handsome Chicago detective was fast becoming the elephant in the room whenever they were alone. "Okay, look. Here's the thing. He does this, Megs. He falls hard, but he has no staying power and a long-distance relationship is heartbreak waiting to happen. Somebody's going to get hurt and I don't want it to be you." He stopped fidgeting with his napkin and looked her in the eye at last. "He's never going to leave Chicago. Everyone in his family from his grandfather to his little sister are cops. He loves the force. Are you willing to move to Chicago to be with him?"

Oh, dear Lord, he was serious. While she'd been considering inviting Vin down to River's Edge to see if this thing with him was anything at all, Sean had them uprooting their lives to be together. She gazed at him, trying to see what was going on in that hard Irish head of his. Was he worrying about what effect a relationship with Vin would have on their friendship? Both hers and his and Vin's and his?

Finally, she sighed. "Look, no one's pulling up stakes here, you big dope. I like the guy. He's sweet and he's smart and he's gorgeous and he likes me. So why not just chill and let me enjoy that, okay?"

Sean's lips twisted briefly before he gave her a smile. "Okay," he said. "Are you going to finish that piece of pie?"

Chapter Six

"C'MON, SAM, HELP me out here." Megan paced the winery tasting room while Sam refilled wine racks from the cases that sat on floor.

"Girl, you are a damn bundle of energy," Sam observed, opening another case. "Here"—she pointed to a cardboard case of Donal's Dream pinot noir—"put it to good use and rack those bottles. Conor and Ali are going to be back from visiting Sean pretty soon and I want to read her a story tonight."

Megan sighed and stooped over the case, pulling bottles and slipping them into the wooden racks lined up on the back wall. "Think of someone."

"Tell me again why we need to find Sean a date?" Sam swiped her forearm across her sweaty face and blew her bangs off her forehead.

"Because Vin is coming this weekend and I don't want us to be a threesome at Dad's for dinner."

"Okay." Sam tapped one sneakered foot on the wide-plank floor. "How about Britney, the art teacher at the elementary school?"

"Um, no."

"Is it because her name is Britney? Because that's not her fault."

Meg raised one brow. "No, it's because she bats for the other team and would have no interest in Sean."

"Seriously?" Sam sat back on her butt and crossed her legs. "Are you sure?"

"I've known Brit since junior high. She's gay. She came out senior year to the surprise of absolutely no one." Megan racked more bottles, turning them so that the front labels were on top just as Char had shown her years ago—the first time she volunteered during the summer rush.

"Huh." Sam pursed her lips and tilted her head. "Okay, moving on." She stowed a few more bottles. "What about Gia Bishop, my new paralegal? She's been divorced a while, she's cute, and as far as I know she's not dating anyone yet. She'd be perfect for Sean because she's new in town, so no skeevy high-school memories."

Megan snapped her fingers. "Oh, yeah! Hey, she's sweet and just Sean's type—smart, tiny, brunette, and juggy." She curved her hands in front of her chest. "She'll be perfect! Will you talk to her?"

Sam rose to her feet in one smooth move that Megan couldn't help admiring and envying just a little bit. She'd never been able to do that, not even when she was a teenager—something about balance and having bodacious boobs. "*I* have to talk to her?"

"She's your friend."

"She's also my employee." Sam carted several empty boxes to the stairwell beside the office. "Would asking if she wanted to be fixed up cross some kind of line?"

Megan shook her head. "Nah. It's an all-female office; you're friends. Wait until you're on a break or after hours to talk to her."

"Do you really want to double with Sean and a blind date on one of the two nights you're going to have with *Vincenzo*?" Sam grinned and faked a swoon.

"Why do you insist on calling him that?" Megan gathered up her hair and swirled it into a messy knot on her head with the elastic hair band she kept around her wrist almost continually.

Sam gave her a wide-eyed look. "It's his name, isn't it?"

"Yes, but it's how you say it. Like he's some kind of Italian romance novel hero." She pulled open another case and slid more bottles into the racks.

"Wait! That's zin—it goes over here." Sam pointed. "And Vin *is* an Italian romantic hero—at least as close to one as we'll see here in River's Edge. Because we sure can't count old Mario Moretti, even though his pizzas are to die for."

"No, we can't," Megan agreed. "He has hair in his ears."

Vin, on the other hand, truly did qualify as a romantic hero, and he was doing his very best to prove it to her. After all, how often did a mayor get flowers delivered to her office in town hall twice in as many weeks? She smiled as she thought about the pink roses that had arrived just that morning—how could he possibly have known pink was her favorite color of roses? She'd taken the sunflowers home to use as a centerpiece, shaking a finger at Mamie to remind her to stay away from them. Mamie merely gazed at her in that inscrutable way cats had. Yeah, Vincenzo DeLuca was romancing the heck out of her and she loved every moment of it.

Sam's chuckle brought her out of her reverie and when Megan looked up, her friend was grinning.

"What?" Megan got busy again emptying the case of zin in to the proper racks.

Sam shook her head and clucked her tongue. "You are a goner, my friend."

"You should talk, lady." Meg tossed her a withering glance. "You and Conor glow every time you're together."

"Yeah, we do, don't we?" Sam managed to look delighted and chagrined all at one time.

Megan was truly happy for her new friend, not only because Sam had found the love of her life in Conor Flaherty, but also because she'd also found two new careers in River's Edge. Sam had stepped right into the role of little Ali Flaherty's mom like she'd been born to it, and she'd taken to Harry Evans's law practice as if she'd been there all her life. Meg knew that Sam already loved River's Edge and all its quirky citizens; in turn, they'd fallen in love with Sam Hayes, who was soon to become Sam Flaherty.

Conor and Sam had already booked Dykeman's Orchard for a late-September wedding, the details of which they'd gratefully put into event planner Leigh Dykeman's capable hands. The wedding was tucked tidily into the schedule between picking early- and late-harvest varietals, but if the weather didn't cooperate, the honeymoon would simply have to happen later, after harvest and winemaking season was over. Dykeman's was their choice because Conor and Emmy, his first wife who had died three years earlier, had gotten married at Four Irish Brothers Winery. He wanted this new life with Sam to start in a new place. Sam had confided her relief about that one night over wine and cheese at Sam's little apartment above the law offices, and Meg didn't blame her a bit. Stepping into Emmy Flaherty's life was going to be hard enough on her new friend—how kind of Conor to do what he could to ease Sam's way.

The yellow dress Megan would be wearing when she stood next to Sam as maid of honor already hung in Meg's closet. Sean would be best man since Bren had been best man when Conor married Emmy. Megan loved weddings and, although this one would be a simple affair, she was still excited to be a part of it. Even though the nuptials were weeks away, she'd already been considering asking Vin if he wanted to come down from Chicago and be her date. Well, she'd wait until after the coming weekend before she antici- pated the wedding. But still, how fun would it be to see her gorgeous cop all dressed up in a suit and then to be the one removing it later?

"What are you thinking about?" Sam stacked empty cases and added them to the ones she intended to carry downstairs. "You've got a faraway look in your eyes and you just licked your lips. Were you daydreaming about something delicious, like chocolate lava cake or your dad's French onion soup? Or possibly a certain hot, hot police detective?"

Megan had the grace to blush as she loaded her last empty wine box onto the pile by the stairs. "I was thinking about inviting Vin to be my plus-one at your wedding. I mean if this weekend turns out okay and he's still interested when he sees me in person again."

"Oh, come on, Megs—he's seen you on FaceTime almost every night for the last eight weeks."

"I know, but that's mostly my face. What if he doesn't remember that I'm curvy and that I don't have the tiny butt most men dream of?" Megan tried, but failed to keep the wistful tone out of her voice.

"Trust me, he remembers and he's dying to get his hands on you."

"How do *you* know?" Meg challenged.

Sam sighed. "Because I've seen how practically every man in town over the age of fifteen drools over your butt whenever you walk down the street. You're JLo, for Pete's sake. Nobody forgets a bod like yours, my friend." She shook her head. "I'm sure Vin has been fantasizing about the moment he'll get you all to himself this weekend." Sam shoved the pile of boxes and followed them as they tumbled down the concrete steps to the cellar floor.

With a quick glance at her watch, Megan hurried after her so they could stack them in the storeroom. It was nearly time for Ali to go to bed, so Sam needed to get the winery closed up. Besides, Megan wanted to fly by Char's and see how Sean was doing with his new immobilizer. She had a surprise in her car for him—something she believed he'd truly get a kick out of.

"OH, MY GOD, you brought me a walking stick!" Sean grinned at Megan as he pushed up from the leather club chair in Char's cozy living room. Tentatively, he leaned on the ebony stick, fingering the brass head that fit perfectly in his hand and testing his balance. What an awesome find! Trust Megs to scope out something that made needing a cane seem way cooler than it actually was.

"Do you love it?" Megan offered her arm as he took one tentative step, but he shook his head to let her know he was fine on his own.

He walked the ten or so steps to the front door and then back to his chair, letting the stick keep him balanced. It was perfect. "I do love it. How did you ever think of this?" Easing back into the chair, he put his air-cast-clad healing leg on the ottoman and examined the wooden body of the stick.

Below the brass cap was carved a fascinating tableau of birds, an eagle at the top, an owl, a cardinal, and several other birds—all the way down to the black rubber foot.

"Do you remember when you graduated from law school and a bunch of us went down to Louisville to the Brown Hotel for supper to celebrate and we saw that guy with the curly waxed mustache standing outside the bar?"

Sean thought for a minute before the memory came back to him. "Oh, yeah. He had on a black cutaway jacket and a white vest and gray striped pants."

She nodded. "Yup, and he shook that crazy-ass carved walking stick at us."

Sean chuckled. "Oh that's right. Remember Bren said all he needed was a monocle and he could pass for the Monopoly man." He snapped his fingers as the picture got clearer in his head. "And I said—"

Megan interrupted, her eye sparkling, "You said *I want his walking stick. I'll bet it has a knife stowed in it.*"

How did she remember that? And wouldn't it rock if *this* one had a hidden blade? Sean hefted his new cane, as the fifteen-year-old kid came out in him. "Does this one…"

She shook her head. "Nope. Better than a knife. Unscrew it at that brass ring there." She pointed to a shiny band about five inches below the head of the stick.

Mystified at what could be cooler than a cane with a hidden knife, Sean slid his hand down the warm ebony wood to the brass disk and took the stick apart. At first it appeared hollow, but then he saw something gleaming in the lamp-light. "What the…" He stuck a finger inside and pulled out a glass tube with a brass cap on it. He peered at it for moment. "Is this… is this a *flask*?"

"You bet." Meg chortled. "There's five of 'em in there. Each one holds an ounce and half of whiskey or brandy or even Donal's Dream if that's what your little heart desires."

Sean emptied all five flasks from the cane as warmth washed over him. Only his Megs would think of turning a bitch of a situation into an opportunity to have fun. She was the best. "It's perfect, Meggers, thank you." He held out his arms and she hugged him from her spot on the arm of the big chair, being careful not to put any weight on his lap. Her hair smelled like apricots and a tendril slid across his face when she pressed her cheek to his. At this point, she felt so right against his chest, he wouldn't have cared if she plopped down onto his aching right thigh … and points east.

He sucked in a quick breath. Dear God, did he just have a sexual thought about Megan Mackenzie? Well, hell, maybe she was right. If he was thinking of his old pal in that way, it *had* been too long since he'd had a date. "So who is this woman you and Sam are fixing me up with Friday night?" he asked, trying not to show how bereft he felt when she'd pulled away and settled onto the sofa across from him.

"It's Sam's new paralegal, Gia Bishop," Megan enthused, her eyes alight. "She's sweet and smart and damn pretty. Just your type—dark hair, dark eyes, and a cute little figure. Big boobs, exactly like all the girls I've ever seen you date."

"I don't have a *type*," Sean denied hotly as he started putting the glass tubes back into the walking stick.

"Oh, puhleez, you so have a type." Megan crossed her arms over her chest and looked down her pert little nose at him. "Name me one person you've ever dated who weighed more than a hundred pounds."

"I don't date only one kind of woman! How shallow do you think I am? Size is a stupid criterion for picking a date." He ransacked his brain for at least one woman he'd been with who was as round and lush as Megs. He couldn't think of anyone. *Dammit.*

Megan smirked. "It is, but it's clearly your measure, not mine."

"Um, excuse me, but name me one guy you've ever dated who wasn't at least six feet tall and two hundred twenty pounds." It was feeble, but he needed to defend himself at some level.

"That's entirely different." Megan replied, skewering him with a narrow-eyed glare. "I *do* pick guys who are bigger than me. It's my female prerogative. Do you have any idea how embarrassing it is to be a woman and be the hefty one in a relationship? Society frowns, my friend."

"Hefty? You? Really?" Sean couldn't believe she was referring to herself as *hefty*—all he saw were luscious curves and breasts that made most men's mouths water. He blinked and shook his head to clear those kinds of thoughts from his mind. "And wait a minute. I can't believe my feminist buddy is playing the *female prerogative* card. Why is *my* male prerogative to choose brunettes who are tiny and have big boobs any less valid?"

Megan threw up her hands. "Okay, I surrender. This isn't a hill I want to die on tonight. All I'm saying is I think you'll like Gia. You two have a lot in common. There's the legal thing and she likes music from the eighties like you do and Sam says she loves your brother's summer wines."

Sean grinned. He'd missed this back-and-forth with Megs since he'd moved away. Some of the best times of his youth had been spent wrangling politics and feminism with her over pizza at Mario's or while they pruned vines for Da. He knew exactly what buttons to push to get her riled and often took the opposite side of an issue just to hear her passionate defense of the side he was actually on in the first place. She should've been an attorney, but she made a hell of a great accountant and a dandy mayor. Everyone in River's Edge adored and trusted her.

"What are you grinning at, you big doofus?" Megan shoved the wisp of a curl that had escaped her messy bun behind her ear.

He gulped as, in spite of his grin, a lump suddenly formed in his throat, something that seemed to be happening all too frequently lately. "Have I told you how glad I am to be healing here at home and how much I appreciate your friendship?"

Her eyes softened and a hint of a smile appeared. "Awww, thanks, buddy. I appreciate you, too." She played it little-girl shy, which sent a shaft of tenderness through him.

This whole sentimental thing that had risen inside him since the shooting befuddled the hell out of him. His throat closed whenever one of his brothers hugged him or when Char dropped a kiss on his hair as she passed him at the breakfast table or when little Ali cooed over his cast and touched it with tiny gentle fingers. He had to swallow hard when Mac stopped by his booth at the Riverside to pat his shoulder or when Dot or Noah popped out of their shops to say hello as he wheeled by. Last week, he'd nearly lost it when Frank and Tierney Ashton stopped by the PT room to check in just because they were in the health center anyway on an EMT run. Tears stung his eyelids so often anymore, he was tempted to start carrying a big white handkerchief like Vinnie did. *Sheesh.*

He blinked and cleared his throat. Time to get this conversation back round to their old teasing tenor before he broke down and cried like a baby. "Why are you dragging me and a blind date along on your first night with Vin anyway? From what he's been texting, seems like he'll be glad to see me for like ten minutes. The rest of the weekend he's expecting to *be* with you." He waggled his brows hoping to get a chuckle out of her.

She didn't even crack a smile.

He gave it another shot, offering up a second dose of

Groucho Marx. "He even booked a room at the no-tell motel up on the highway, which tells me he doesn't expect to stay in a motel up on the highway…"

Nada.

"Okay. What's the problem?" He couldn't figure out her troubled expression.

Wasn't Vinnie's arrival in River's Edge the fulfillment of her every dream for the last couple of months? Seeing Megs again was certainly Vinnie's fondest wish.

"Sean, I'm scared." She looked up, fear evident in her eyes. "I really like this guy. I mean I *really* like him. He's smart and funny and kind and well… Okay, maybe I'm as shallow as you, he's gorgeous. I know we hardly know each other, but I want to know him better. See what comes of this." She clasped her hands together under her chin. "Your brothers said he's a player though. Do you think he's just playing with me? What if I'm just another notch on a handsome cop's… I dunno… nightstick?"

Sean couldn't help it. He tried to swallow the guffaw, but he burst out laughing. "Ha! Nice one!"

She gave him a long-suffering eye roll. "You know what I mean."

"Look, Vin falls in love at the drop of a hat, but maybe you're the woman who can make him stay focused. He sure seems to be chasing you." He pointed one long finger at her. "Case in point? How many times has he texted you today alone?"

Meg blushed adorably. "I dunno. Several."

"More than ten?"

"Probably," she confessed, her cheeks pinkening even more.

"Don't sweat it." Sean took a long sip from the water bottle that accompanied him everywhere. The physical therapist had told him to get at least sixty-four ounces in a day for healing and double that for strength. So he drank water—a lot. "Who knows? You could be his Annette Bening."

She frowned. "His *who?*"

Sean sighed. "Do you know who Warren Beatty is?"

"That name sounds familiar..." Megan's brow furrowed further. "Isn't he an actor?"

"Okay, obviously, I've been watching too many old movies with Char. Yes, he's an actor, who made a ton of movies back in the seventies and eighties and nineties. Had a reputation for being a real player. But he finally settled down when he was like in his fifties and married Annette Bening. They met when they were in a movie called *Bugsy* together, and they've been married ever since."

She snapped her fingers. "I know *Bugsy*. Dad loves that movie. Those two are married now?"

"Yep, for like over twenty-five years." He held out his hands. "So see? You could be Annette to Vinnie's Warren."

Her face wreathed in smiles. "Ya think?"

"Sure, why not?" It took everything he had to smile back

at her because he knew Vinnie. Once he got Meg into bed, his interest would wane. Vin was all about the chase. He always had been. But Sean supposed it was possible that Megan Mackenzie could be the woman who brought Vin DeLuca to heel. Stranger things had happened. Maybe Meg and Vin were destined for true love.

However, Sean hoped not.

Chapter Seven

SEAN STEERED THE golf cart up through the vineyard, delighted to be outside on his own. "Dude!" he called when he was nearly even with the row of vines where Conor was working. "Check me! I'm driving!"

Shoving his big sunhat off his forehead, Conor grinned. "Hey, look at you!" He dropped into the seat next to Sean, released a huge sigh, and glanced at the little cooler that sat on the back of the cart. "Got any extra water in there? As Da would say, it's hotter than the hinges of hell out here."

"Water, beer, lunch, and some news." Sean locked the brake, eased out of the seat, and opened the cooler to hand over a water, a frosty bottle of beer, and a square container. "Ham and cheese, compliments of your big brother, who is officially on his own now."

"Oh, man, thanks! Is that your news? I already knew that. Ollie's been gone almost a week." Conor downed the water before he opened the container and took a giant bite of the sandwich.

"Hey, I spent five minutes making that sandwich. I even cut it diagonally, which I'm sure you know is the universal signal of a sandwich made with love. You could at least take a moment to appreciate the beauty of a well-made ham on rye before you scarf it down like a junkyard dog." Sean pulled another sandwich and beer from the cooler and tossed a small bag of chips onto the seat next to his brother. "And no, that's not my news." He settled back behind the wheel of the cart.

"Okay, *somebody's* been watching way too much Food Network. I didn't realize you'd become such a kitchen prima donna since you got home." Conor shoved the rest of the sandwich half into his mouth, his cheeks puffing out like a hamster's.

Sean chose to ignore his little brother's antics. "No, that's still not my news."

"What *is* your news then?" Conor mumbled around a mouthful of ham, provolone, and marble rye.

"I really am on my own now. Char's heading to Florida." Sean took a bite of his own sandwich—roast beef and smoked Gouda on a potato bun. He'd been thoroughly enjoying helping Char in the kitchen the last week or so. Being able to get around and be useful was stimulating, so he'd taken over cooking, making breakfasts and lunches, trying to be creative when he packed her food before she left for work at the Four Irish Brothers tasting room in town. He'd scoured the internet to come up with interesting and delectable dishes for supper, enjoying the challenges that cooking presented.

"Crap. Are you kidding me?" Conor finally swallowed, washing the sandwich down with a slug of beer. "What's going on? Is it Ethel?"

Sean nodded. "The old girl broke her hip." Their step-grandmother was a ninety-three-year-old fireball, who played golf, shelled on the beach every morning, and still tooled around the little Florida gulf coast town of Seaside on a moped. "Hit some sand on the moped and lost control. She's okay, but she's laid up for a few weeks."

"Aw, damn. It was inevitable, the way she blasts around town on that stupid scooter." Conor wiped sweat off his brow with a crumpled paper towel from his shorts pocket. "She's okay though?"

"Yeah." Sean took a long pull on his beer. "Char's been trying to get her off that thing for months now, but she said Ethel just laughs and guns her engine, such as it is. Ethel's already warned her nobody better think of selling it while she's in the rehab."

"When's Char taking off?" Conor sounded dubious.

Clearly, he was worrying about who was going to run the tasting room on the riverfront that had always been their stepmother's territory. Sean didn't blame him for being concerned. Only two of the summer kids who helped in the vineyard were old enough to pour tastings and even then, they had to have an adult over twenty-one on the premises while they poured.

"She takes off from Louisville tomorrow morning. I'm

paying Nate to take her to the airport, and I've arranged for a rental car for her in Florida. She thinks she'll be down there at least a month." Sean adjusted his position to make his immobilized thigh a bit more comfortable. "I can run the tasting room for you until she gets back. It'll be good for me to be busy and out among people again."

At least that's what the shrink would say.

He'd been seeing Lianne Morrison, the psychologist, once a week since he'd gotten home even though he didn't think he'd been having any traumatic reaction to the shooting. Well, except for the nightmares that woke him shivering and sweating at least twice a week. Always the same terrifying dream in which someone he loved was being chased by a masked gunman. It didn't take Sigmund Freud to figure that one out. Dr. Morrison had hinted that his easy tendency toward tears was related to the shooting as well, but Sean believed it was simply relief at being home among his tribe. Chicago was high-octane and his work was interesting, if exhausting, but he'd missed his brothers, his hometown, and the verdant hills of southern Indiana.

Becoming a partner in the firm two years ago had been the highlight of his career, but the shine had worn off that particular brass ring. Caseloads had gotten heavier with more and more contentious divorces occurring, and the tough ones seemed to fall to him. Sean often worked long hours, coming home late at night to drop into bed with no time to truly enjoy the fruits of his labor. His housecleaners spent more time in his beautiful modern apartment that overlooked Lake Michigan than he did, and he still had to toss drawers and cupboards every now and then, trying to find things that the decorator had tucked away when she and her team renovated the pricey place a couple of years ago.

The only entertainment in his life in the big city was playing poker every other Friday night with Vinnie and his cop buddies, and wasn't that a sad state of affairs? He was thirty-eight years old and living like a monk because work had become his entire life.

Sean stared out across the vineyard as he munched on his sandwich, enjoying the Indiana summer sun, the buzz of the bees flying around the vines, and the view of the Ohio River flowing lazily along far below. The swelling lump in his throat at the thought of leaving soon was such a visceral reaction, he closed his eyes and swallowed against it. A tap on his wrist brought him back to the golf cart and his brother.

"Hey? You okay?" Conor had already devoured his sandwich and started on the bag of chips.

Sean blinked and returned his focus. "Sorry. Yeah, I'm fine. Just enjoying the view." He leaned back against the cushioned seat and set his right leg up on the dashboard to rest it. He was glad to be in the immobilizer now and able to remove it for showers and when the wound started to itch too bad to bear. The thigh was wicked ugly, but he was upright and walking, and the PT assured him the scar would eventually fade. "Man, Da and Ma sure picked an amazing spot, didn't they?"

Conor gave him a curious glance before staring out across the landscape. "They did. See that field down there? The one Mike used to rent for alfalfa?" He pointed.

Sean sighted along Conor's finger to an overgrown five acres below them. He remembered Conor saying after Mike died that he was going to let it go fallow until he decided what to do with it. "Yeah. Did anyone take it over for you?"

"Nah, Nate's been mowing now and then since Mike passed. But I'm thinking about planting some Frontenac vines down there." Conor took a drink of beer. "It's a sturdy grape that can take our winters. I had a couple of awesome Frontenac rosés at Purdue last May and a port that knocked my socks off."

"Isn't that a highly acidic grape?" Sean had been reading voraciously from his father's library of wine books since he'd been home, at first because he was bored; but the more he read, the more fascinated he'd become.

Conor's dark brows furrowed. "Yeah, it is and it's high in sugar when it ripens midseason, which makes it better for blending, but we could do amazing things with rosés and Da's port recipe. It's pretty hardy and disease resistant, so I think we should give it try."

A surge of pride swelled in Sean's chest. His little brother had kept Four Irish Brothers going and even made it a destination winery in the Midwest with his savvy handling of the grapes and the business. His summertime pizza-and-wine nights drew crowds from as far away as Louisville and Indianapolis, much to the delight of the rest of the River's Edge. Restaurant and shop owners loved the tourists he was bringing in, as did the three B and Bs in town and the two hotels. Chautauqua in the fall always brought lots of people to River's Edge, but the Southern Indiana Wine Trail was increasing traffic all year long, and Four Irish Brothers was a favorite on the tour.

He bumped shoulders with Conor. "Sounds good to me. You're the winemaker. I trust your judgment." He reached for the new walking stick he'd placed behind the seat of the golf cart. "Speaking of port, check this out."

Conor took the stick. "This is awesome! You and Harry can joust on the town square." He brandished the cane like a sword. "You better watch him though. I've heard his cane actually has a real sword in it."

Sean retrieved his walking stick and turned the top at the brass ring. "Big deal. Mine has something way better than a knife." He unscrewed the top, tipped out a glass tube filled with rich dark red liquid, and held it up.

Conor opened the tube and sniffed. "Holy crap! A flask! Is that Da's Ruby Harbor?" He sipped from the tube, then closed his eyes in apparent ecstasy. "It is!"

Sean retrieved the tube and sipped, too. "Yup. I've got five of those in this thing. Is that cool or what?"

"Where did you find a walking stick with flasks in it?"

Conor peered into the body of the cane. "You're right, this is way better than a sword. And much more practical."

Sean grinned. "Megs brought it to me last night."

"That woman is the best."

"She is, isn't she?" Sean held the flask up to let the sunlight shimmer through the wine, wondering what Megan would think when he showed her how he'd filled the flasks. It could be an icebreaker tonight if the conversation lagged, which was highly unlikely if Vinnie DeLuca was involved.

He was nervous about the blind date, but he would never admit it to anyone, not even his brother. His dating skills were rusty as hell and not only because of the shooting. Spending twelve hours a day at work and his policy never to go out with anyone from the office had put dating on the back burner. Vin had fixed him up now and again, but because he couldn't devote time to nurturing a relationship, things fizzled out quickly.

This blind date would probably not come to anything either, because Gia lived here and he was headed back to Chicago in a few weeks. On the other hand, look at Vin and Megs… or *don't*. That image sent an arc of resentment through him, although he couldn't say why. For reasons that he was attributing to the shooting, he didn't want to share his life in River's Edge with anyone from Chicago, not even his good buddy, Vin. And Meg was part of home, not Chicago.

Conor nabbed the tube and sipped again. "Damn, that's

good stuff. We're down to about fifteen cases of this one, so I took it off the tasting menu. But Da's Ruby Reserve has been in oak bourbon barrels for the last five years and we've been blending, so it's about ready to bottle. That and the zin."

"How soon?" Sean hoped he'd be there to help bottle. He'd missed working in the wine cellar. He hadn't ruined a pair of running shoes in longer than he could remember.

"Probably in the next month or so." Conor handed him the flask, hopped out of the golf cart, and clamored into a dusty green Gator—the utility vehicle he used to get around in the vineyard. "Hey, follow me up to the barn and we'll barrel taste it. I'd love to see what you think. If you're going to be pouring tastings, you'll be pushing this one soon. I'd like to get it out for fall."

A frisson of pleasure swept through Sean as he put the cart in gear and bumped through the vineyard to the winery. He shoved all the disturbing thoughts about his two friends getting together to the back of his mind. His confused feelings about Meg and Vinnie were probably fodder for a session with Dr. Morrison anyway. Right now, the sun was shining, he was in his favorite place in all the world, and he was sharing some damn good port with his brother. Nothing else mattered.

"ALI, SWEETIE, DON'T mess with Aunt Megan's makeup,"

Sam called from her perch on the side of Megan's bed.

Megan glanced at the nook that housed her sink and vanity, her heart swelling at the sight of Conor's five-year-old daughter examining the tubes and containers of lipstick and eye shadow spread across the counter.

Ali picked up a bottle of cologne and sniffed the atomizer. "This smells like flowers, Aunt Meg."

"You want some on you?" Megan glanced in the closet mirror before trotting over to the vanity. "Here, let me show you a fun trick." She sprayed some of the light floral cologne in the air and walked through the mist, then sprayed behind her and backed up, letting the cologne drift over her.

"Oh, do me!" Ali clasped her hands in delight. "Is it okay, Sam? Even if I'm not a grown-up lady yet?"

Sam chuckled. "Of course it's okay, honey. Even little girls like to smell nice."

Megan misted the air and Ali danced through, sniffing, then coughing a little as she got showered with the scent of violets and apricots and a hint of citrus. "Oooh, that's so pretty. I smell like a lady now."

"Da's going to love it." Sam held out her arms and Ali rushed into them.

Megan felt a lump rise in her throat. Sam was a natural mother and Meg couldn't deny her own biological clock nudged her every so often, even more frequently since Sam had arrived and fallen in love with Conor and Ali. She turned and gazed at herself in the closet mirror, smoothing one manicured hand over the front of her dress, and for the briefest of moments imagined her belly round with Vin's baby. A dark-haired, dark-eyed little charmer with Vin's gorgeous looks and her gift for math.

She shook her head. How stupid. This was only her fourth real date with a guy she'd known just a few weeks. She wasn't even sure she was falling in love with Vin. Lust, absolutely, but love? At thirty-seven, she should know what it felt like to fall passionately in love, shouldn't she?

She scowled at her reflection. "Is this sundress going to be okay? Not too much skin?"

Sam tossed Ali on the bed and nuzzled her ear while the kid giggled and threw her arms around Sam's neck. When she sat up, she pulled Ali close and eyed Megan's flowered sundress. A flowing skirt fell gracefully from the empire waistline and narrow shoulder straps crisscrossed over the low-cut back revealing the fact that she wasn't wearing a bra. "It's perfect—sexy, but not too much of anything. It's July, for cripe's sake. You'll swelter at the concert this evening if you wear more. Take a sweater for the diner, though. You know your dad. He's always got the AC set to arctic."

"Thank heaven for built-in bras or I'd never be able to pull off this look." Megan twirled in front of the mirror, enjoying the silky feel of the fabric against her calves.

"You look be-yooooo-tiful, Aunt Meg!" Ali cuddled into the crook of Sam's arm. "Uncle Sean is going to love you."

Megan tugged the little girl's braid. "It's not Uncle Sean

MEANT TO BE

I'm trying to impress, kiddo."

Ali scrunched up her button nose. "I thought you were going out with Uncle Sean tonight. That's what Da said."

"Well, my friend Vin and I are double-dating with Uncle Sean and Gia Bishop—you know Gia. She works with Sam."

"What's a double date?" Ali fidgeted with her braid.

"When two couples go out together for a date, that's called double-dating," Sam explained patiently while Megan took one last look in the vanity mirror and applied a tinge more lip gloss. "Aunt Megan's date is Vin and Uncle Sean's date is Gia."

"Well, that's not right," Ali declared. "Aunt Meg belongs with Uncle Sean."

The bald statement intrigued Meg. "Why do you think that?"

"'Cause he's *Uncle* Sean and you're *Aunt* Meg," the child explained with exaggerated patience. "Aunts and uncles go together."

Megan met Sam's eyes over Ali's dark head as they both tried not to chuckle. How could she argue with five-year-old logic like that? "Well, hon, who knows? Maybe one day, you'll have Aunt Meg and Uncle Vin."

"Nah. That sounds weird." Ali rose from the bed and twirled in front of the mirror as she'd seen Megan do earlier, the matter clearly closed in her estimation. "My dress doesn't puff out like yours does." She pouted.

Sam got up too and held out her hand to her soon-to-be

stepdaughter. "Your skirt is too straight to puff out, sweetie, but we can go home and check your closet for one that will. Then you can twirl for Da."

"I bet my pink one with the bunny on it will!" Ali scampered to the door, ignoring Sam's hand.

Sam gave Meg a quick hug. "Have fun tonight and you better be prepared to share details on Sunday night after he leaves." She shook her finger and grinned.

A rush of affection surged through Meg as she returned the hug. How lucky she was to have found such a good friend in Conor Flaherty's new love. "A full report, I promise."

They left and she turned to her dresser to find a lightweight sweater to throw around her shoulders if it got too chilly in the diner after the concert on the square.

Her heart was in her throat at the thought of seeing Vin again, but excitement and—okay, she'd admit it—*lust* shivered through her when she pictured the sexy police detective who'd been wooing her with such panache via emails, FaceTime calls, and texts. She wandered into the living room to peer out the big front window that overlooked her dad's backyard and house when her phone chimed in the small clutch she'd chosen to carry on her date. She pulled it out and swiped the screen.

"Hey, gorgeous. At the light in the center of town. ETA 6:43 per GPS."

Her breath caught. He was four minutes away. They'd only have time for a quick hello before they had to pick up

Sean and Gia and get to the square for the oldies concert. Seating at the summer concerts on the square was usually first come, first served, but she didn't want Sean to have to stand for very long, so she'd played her mayor card earlier in the day and reserved seats for the four of them near the bandstand.

She flipped on a lamp, took one last look at her freshly cleaned apartment, and stepped out, deciding to meet Vin down in the driveway. They'd have plenty of time for her to show him the apartment later. Butterflies flitted through her belly. If she was reading Vin correctly, chances were very good that the only room they'd be in tonight would be her bedroom.

Heart pounding, she took a deep breath as a late-model SUV pulled into the driveway and the man himself stepped out of the car, looking even more beautiful than she remembered. She smiled as he sauntered to her. Without a word, he drew her to him and kissed her full on the lips. Heat shimmered through her as she opened her lips to his seeking tongue. Dear Lord, how she'd missed him.

Apparently he had missed her, too, and his urgent kisses sent ripples of sensation right to her core. *Aunt Megan and Uncle Vin* indeed.

Chapter Eight

M EGAN TOYED WITH her salad, shifting a succulent piece of grilled salmon under a chunk of avocado that had been seared on her dad's big outdoor grill set up in the courtyard between the diner and Clyde Schwimmer's Antiques and Uniques. They'd opted to eat outside in the courtyard, what Mac referred to as his *al fresco dining room.* Every summer, he filled the long narrow space with tables and chairs, raised umbrellas over the seating, and strung lights between the buildings to create as much of a Paris outdoor café vibe as he could for his patrons.

The salad was delicious as always—a perfectly rendered Caesar coated with Mac's famous dressing and served with a warm French baguette. Sean had ordered a bottle of Four Irish Brothers gewürztraminer, while Vin had opted for Chianti, so two bottles of wine were open at their table. Usually, Megan loved eating under the stars, watching her father create incredible dishes on the grill, enjoying the murmur of conversations at other tables while she sipped a crisp summer white wine.

Usually.

But tonight, her stomach roiled, a dull ache was developing in the back of her neck, and her chest hurt. Her dream date had turned into a nightmare, and all she wanted was to escape to her quiet apartment, to Mamie's sweet, soothing purr, and the slice of Paula's French silk pie that was waiting in her fridge.

The evening had started out exactly as she'd hoped— Vin's strong arms around her, his lips warm and delectable on hers. When they pulled apart, the look of hunger in his dark eyes sent a spasm of longing right to her core. She'd fought the urge to simply text Sean and Gia to go on without them. But the fact was she and Vin were picking them up, so after one more passionate kiss, Vin turned her toward the car and they headed for Sean's.

Sean and Vin greeted each other like long-lost brothers, bro-hugging and slapping one another on the back while Megan watched from the front seat. No question how much they'd missed each other. Sean slid into the back of Vin's SUV with no problems and gave her shoulder a quick squeeze before they drove back into town to pick up Gia.

Yeah. Gia.

Megan glanced up at the lovely Gia Bishop, who sat to her left and was currently involved in yet another animated discussion with Vin, this time about Italy. Turned out her maiden name, which she was thinking of taking back since her divorce, was Rosetti and her family was from the same area of northern Italy that Vin's family was from.

And wouldn't you just know it?

Her aunt was married to a DeLuca, so she and Vin were sharing family histories over Mac's delicately sauced chicken tetrazzini. Megan had already heard more than she ever wanted to know about Savigliano, Italy, and the fact that Gia's extremely short sundress, which exposed her skinny shoulders and emphasized her great boobs, was made from fabric that was manufactured in the silk mill where Vin's great-grandfather had once worked.

How lovely.

The coincidences had been coming on strong all evening long. Gia was not only Italian, incredibly beautiful, and tiny with a face that stopped traffic, but she was also the daughter, granddaughter, sister, and niece of a family of Cincinnati cops. Turned out Vin knew her dad from an interstate investigation they'd cooperated on a couple of years earlier.

Go figure.

They both played softball—Vin played on Chicago's 12th district team with his brothers and cousins, while Gia had just started coaching the peewee team at the River's Edge Little League field near the east end of town. They both *loved* Italian wine and, although Megan wasn't aware that Sangiovese was the most widely cultivated grape in Italy, both Vin and Gia knew that and more, and wasn't it a shame that Mac didn't have any in his wine cellar right then.

Boohoo.

In fact, Vin and Sean's date had talked nonstop almost from the time they'd settled into their seats at the concert on the square. At first, the four of them had laughed at how much Vin and Gia had had in common, but now three hours into the most arduous evening of her life, Megan was over it. When she met Sean's eyes, he merely shrugged and raised one brow. But why should *he* be bothered by Vin and Gia's more-than-obvious attraction to one another? He had no stake in this evening.

To be fair, he'd tried more than once to bring the conversation around to Megan's work as mayor and how much River's Edge had prospered since she'd been elected four years ago. He'd asked Megan about what was happening with the old abandoned cotton mill down by the river—a project near and dear to her heart and one she'd been working on since her election. But after the briefest acknowledgment, Gia and Vin had spent the rest of the concert intermission in a lively debate about who was the greatest Italian opera composer, Rossini or Puccini.

And that fascinating discussion is still going on two hours later. Yawn.

Megan hated opera. Truth was she wasn't even that crazy about musicals, and when she said she'd never seen *Phantom of the Opera*, both Vin and Gia had looked at her like she had carrots sprouting out of her ears before continuing their conversation.

Draining her glass of wine, she looked pointedly at Vin, whose attention was totally focused on Gia's animated story about being at the opening night of *Phantom* at the Cadillac

Palace Theatre in Chicago.

Oh, amazeballs—another coinkydink. Vin was there that night, too.

She pushed back from the table. "Excuse me, I'm going to go to the ladies' room."

Vin glanced up. "Sure."

Gia never took her eyes off Vinnie, so Megan didn't even bother to ask if she needed to join her.

Sean reached for the walking stick he'd leaned against the brick wall behind their table. "Hold on, Meg, I'll walk in with you. I need to stretch this leg a little."

SEAN DIDN'T NEED the rigid set of Megan's shoulders as she strode in front of him to realize how angry his friend was. He didn't blame her one bit, but the look of utter devastation on her face when they finally got into the kitchen of the diner made his heart ache. He glanced around, then herded her into her dad's small office and shut the door.

She dropped into one of the two chairs in the tiny cubicle and covered her face with her hands. "God, is this a nightmare or what?" Her voice was muffled and shaky.

Sean rested against the edge of Mac's cluttered desk, his walking stick between his legs. His thigh throbbed from sitting in the same position for such a long time, even though he'd been stretching it best he could under the table. "Well, this evening's not turning out quite the way we expected, is it?"

"Gee, ya think?" Megan sat back in the chair and expelled a long breath. Then she pointed one finger at him. "And if you say *I told you so*, Sean Flaherty, I swear I'll beat you with that stick."

Sean fought the grin and simply held up his hands, palms forward. "I'm not saying anything," he said, "except I'm so sorry, Megs."

"How did this happen? When did I lose control of this date?" She slumped back into the chair, raking her fingers through her blond curls as tears shimmered in her honey-brown eyes. "When he picked me up, we were fine. I mean we were *hot*. Hell, I should've just gone with my instincts and taken him upstairs right then and there."

Sean's gut clenched. Thank heaven she hadn't slept with Vinnie. If she'd taken him upstairs, Vin would've gotten what he'd been salivating after for eight weeks, and Meg would still be brokenhearted. Well, eventually, when she figured out his buddy had no staying power. The guy didn't mean to be a butt. He just loved women and generally women loved him right back. Most of the time though, the ladies he dated figured out fast that he was incapable of any kind of enduring relationship and bolted before he could break their hearts, which was why Vin always claimed the women were the ones doing the damage.

But it was Meg's heart breaking now and Sean longed to go out and throat-punch Vinnie. However, that would serve no purpose because Vinnie, as smart as he was in so many ways, would have no idea why his attraction to Gia would upset Megan. In Vinnie's world, all women were there to love, and there was no reason he couldn't love both Meg and Gia. Sean had seen the scenario at least half a dozen times since he'd met Vin eight years ago. The handsome cop could rip the heart right out of a trusting, good woman and still play the hapless victim when things finally blew up. Sean would've warned her back in Chicago if he'd believed things would get this far.

Meg sniffled, swiping the back of her hand over her cheek. "Your brothers tried to warn me, but did I listen?" She accepted a tissue from the box Sean had found on the desk, then scraped her off her face again. "Idiot."

He shook his head with regret. "He's clueless, Meg. He thinks women destroy *him* when, in fact, he just doesn't see why he can't have all the women he wants. He's gone through at least three of our paralegals and two servers at my favorite restaurant. He simply doesn't get it."

"Stop making excuses for him. He's a *snake*." Meg blew her nose and reached for another tissue. "How does he live with himself?"

"I'm not making excuses, I'm just telling you how it is and—" Sean bit back the rest because it was only going to come out as *I told you so* and he wasn't interested in being beaten about the head and shoulders with his own cane.

"Your date's no prize either," Meg pointed out, jerking a

thumb toward the courtyard where chances were good Vin and Gia had barely noticed their absence. "Do you think she even realizes *you* were the person she was supposed to be with tonight?"

Sean chuckled. "I doubt she realizes I'm even along. Once she saw Vinnie da Cop, all bets were off for me."

"You seem remarkably unfazed by that."

"Unlike you, I came into tonight with no expectations." He shrugged, wanting to say more, but at the moment, discretion seemed like the better part of valor, so he kept quiet.

Megan sighed deeply. "Dammit. I really thought…"

"You thought he was the one," Sean finished for her.

"*You* even said he could be."

He nodded. "I know. But, honestly, I was only trying to make you feel good. Vinnie's never the one. Not for any-one."

She gave him a hard stare. "Don't you ever do that again, Sean Flaherty. Trying to spare my feelings." She shook her head. "That isn't how we work. We never have."

He offered a smile, but she wasn't having it.

"Get that smirk off your face, you jerk." She sat straight up. "You *knew* what he was and you let me moon around like a damn high-school freshman for the past two months. God, what if I'd slept with him tonight?" Closing her eyes, she shuddered.

Taken aback by the intensity of her tone, he switched to

a scowl. "*I let you?* You want to tell me how I was supposed to stop you? And that wasn't a smirk. I was attempting to smile at you. You know, to try to make you feel better."

They glared at one another for a moment before she had the decency to look abashed. "I'm sorry. I know it's not your fault."

Sean held out his hand to help her out of the chair. "Come on. Go to the restroom and fix your raccoon eyes. I'll go out and tell him I'm walking you home and then—"

"Hell no!" Ignoring his hand, Meg stood up and tossed the tissue box back on the desk. Throwing her shoulders back, she smoothed her dress over her shapely breasts and straightened to her full height.

A quiver of something Sean couldn't quite define went through him. It almost felt like… like *lust*. But before he could examine the sensation in too great of detail, she touched his arm.

"Thanks, buddy, but *I'll* go tell him I'm going home." She marched to the door, yanked it open, and stepped into the steamy kitchen. "And he can just deal with my raccoon eyes. I don't give a crap."

When she turned to look back over her shoulder at him, her blond curls tumbling around her face and her shoulders squared, she appeared for the all world like a glorious warrior princess heading into battle. "Are you coming?"

He pulled himself off the desk. "Are you kidding? I wouldn't miss this for the world."

Chapter Nine

T HE SILENCE WAS killing him. Meg hadn't said more than six words since they'd left the diner. Not on the walk to her apartment, not while they piled into her ancient Honda Accord. Nada. Beyond telling him to feel free to set the seat back if he needed more legroom, she'd been uncharacteristically silent. They were almost to Char's and her lips were still pressed together in a tight line.

Oh, she'd had plenty to say at the diner when they went back out to their table to collect her purse and sweater. Sean chuckled to himself remembering Vinnie's face. The guy had been gobsmacked when Megs lit into him. Using her smiling mayor voice, she'd skinned him alive, riding over his protestations of innocence, while Gia shrank back into her chair and cringed. Meg had ignored Sean's blind date until the very end when she'd simply turned to Gia and said, "Enjoy the rest of *your* date, Gia. You two deserve each other."

Of course Vin was clueless and acted, once again, as if he were the one being wronged. Sean had watched from the steps of the courtyard, not even bothering to say anything to Gia, although their eyes met while Meg shredded Vinnie.

Gia's face showed part terror and part regret, so Sean had simply shrugged his shoulders and given her a brief nod.

He glanced over at Meg, who appeared focused on navigating the curvy driveway into the winery property. "Here's the thing"—he side-eyed her as she pulled into Char's driveway—"Vin is like… like that dog in *Up*."

She switched off the car and turned to face him, her expression incredulous. *"What?"*

"You know the dog in that movie *Up*? We watched it with Ali at Christmas?" His point was valid if she would just open her mind, so he explained further. "The dog had a great ball that he was playing with—having fun, enjoying himself. Loved that ball. Then a squirrel ran by and he was completely distracted, dropped the ball, and chased the squirrel." He grinned, hoping to get some kind of positive reaction.

She rested her elbow on the steering wheel and cupped her chin in her palm. "So, I'm the ball in this scenario?"

"Yeah."

"And Vin is the dog?"

He nodded. She was getting it.

"And Gia is what? The squirrel?"

He threw his hands up in exultation. "Yes, exactly."

She gazed at him for a long moment, "I've heard you say some really dumb stuff over the years, Sean Flaherty, but *that* has to be the dumbest. Stop defending him." She yanked the keys from the ignition and opened her door. "Come on. I'll walk you in."

"I'm not defending him and you're missing the point." Sean sighed and opened his own door, carefully rotating in his seat and setting his cane on the driveway to make sure he was balanced before he got out of the car.

By the time he'd gotten situated, Megan was standing beside the open car door with her elbow crooked. Moonlight streamed through the trees, making a halo of light around her blond curls and emphasizing her soft peachy skin. He took hold of her forearm, and when he rose, they were so close, Sean only had to lean down a fraction of an inch to touch his lips to hers. His breath hitched and he jerked back.

What are you thinking, Flaherty?

She stared at him, her eyes wide. "Okay then, tell me, what's the point?"

She looked so bereft, he couldn't stop himself. He dropped her arm and pulled her into his chest, his hand cupping her head. "The point is," he whispered as the heady scent of her shampoo filled his senses. *Apricots again, and is it roses? Lilacs?* "The point is I'm sorry, Megs. I'm really sorry Vinnie is such a damn jerk."

Wrapping her arms around his waist, she relaxed into him, pressing her face against his knit shirt. They stood that way quietly until Sean realized her shoulders were shaking. He peered down into her face. "Oh, honey, that guy isn't worth a single tear."

"It... it's not h-him." She pulled away, hiccupping and sniffling.

Taking her arm, he brandished his walking stick. "Well, come on in. We'll go out on the screened porch, have a drink, and you can tell me what *it* is. I've got a cane full of port here and even more in a bottle in the house." He turned her toward the front stoop as he shoved the car door closed with his butt.

THE NIGHT BREEZE ruffled Sean's dark hair as he dropped onto the cushioned settee next to her. As a teenager, Megan had been on this porch dozens of times—it was where her group of friends had hung out on summer evenings, listening to music, talking, and sometimes dancing when Sean and the guys shoved the wicker furniture to the edges of the big space. She'd gotten her first real kiss right outside the door, when she and Karl Schwimmer snuck out onto the patio one moonlit June night. Shaking her head, she took a sip of port.

Sean nudged her with his shoulder. "What's that little smile about?"

"Just remembering." Megan sighed and laid her head back on the cushion. "We had a lot of good times out here when we were kids, didn't we?"

He set his glass down on the small table next to the settee. "Remember that night we broke into Da's bottle of Jameson?"

"Oh yeah. You and Karl Schwimmer and Justin

Dykeman and Duane Wilson were all showing off for that new girl." She raked her fingers through her hair to get it off her face. "What was her name?"

Sean chuckled. "Ashley Boggs." He stretched his leg out, resting it on the wicker trunk that had served as a coffee table since Maggie Flaherty's time.

Megan wondered idly why Char hadn't redecorated the porch when she married Donal and moved into the house where he and Maggie had raised their boys. She certainly had made the rest of the place her own. Meg hadn't been in the house all that much since Sean had grown up and moved away. This porch was sweetly reminiscent of her high-school days, which somehow made her all the sadder tonight.

She attempted to shake off the melancholy and gave Sean a smile. "That's right. You idiots drank yourselves sick. Was it you or Duane who hurled on the rug?"

"*That* was Duane. The rest of us had the grace to vomit in the bushes outside." Sean eased his left arm across the back of the settee. "God, Ma was pissed. The four of us had to take the rug outside on the patio and scrub it. She even made us hose down all the bushes back there to get rid of the smell of puke." He tweaked a curl that fell over her cheek. "Good times, eh?"

"Good times." Meg took another sip of port, sighing as she set the glass on the trunk in front of them. When she settled back on the settee, it was the most natural thing in the world to kick off her shoes, curl her legs under her, and cuddle closer to Sean's big body. "Don't kick my glass over," she warned.

"I see it." He lowered his arm and tugged her closer yet.

Megan laid her head on his shoulder and inhaled the essence that had always been Sean Flaherty—sunshine and soap and something green and fresh and woodsy. The ache inside her had waned just a little, but tears still stung her eyes. She swiped at her cheek; she really didn't want to cry anymore. It would be a shame to get mascara all over Sean's soft yellow polo; however when she started to raise her head, he handed her a tissue he'd magically conjured from heaven knew where and his eyes were so full of tenderness, the tears spilled over.

He pressed her back against his chest. "Go ahead and cry it out if you want to." His breath was warm against her temple. "It's okay."

"I don't want to cry anymore. I hate crying over men— it's so useless." She rolled her lips between her teeth and bit down to keep the sobs building in her throat at bay. What was the point of saying you didn't want to cry when you couldn't stop the tears? She swallowed, but the lump remained, so she gave up fighting and bawled like a baby.

He didn't say anything, just rubbed his cheek on her hair while she wept.

At last the storm subsided and she wiped her eyes and blew her nose. "God, Sean, isn't it ever going to be *my* turn?" The words burst out of her with such vehemence, it stunned her.

She clapped a hand over her mouth, horrified the self-pity that had been roaming around in her subconscious for the last couple of years had finally found its voice. Here. Now.

"So that's what *it* is?" Sean slipped one finger under her chin and gazed down into her face, which she was certain looked adorable all tear-stained and raccoon-eyed.

Heat flushed her cheeks, so she pulled away and rested her head on his shoulder again. He waited, idly stroking her arm while she gathered her thoughts.

"I'm so tired of dating. So sick of always thinking, *oh this is good*, and then discovering the guy's a perv or an idiot or just another damn jerk." She sighed and wiped her eyes with the damp tissue.

Sean handed her another one.

"Thanks." She sat up, putting a little space between them. "It isn't that I think I need a man to complete me. I don't. I'm happy with my life, but it gets lonely, you know? And I confess, my biological clock is ticking."

He nodded. "I do know." He pulled her back into the circle of his arm. "Not the biological clock thing, although Ali makes me think about kids. But it gets lonely up in Chicago, too. All I do is work and then I work some more. There's poker with Vin and the guys on Friday nights, and he and I go out for dinner now and again. Frankly, I haven't had an actual date with a woman in longer than I can remember." He grinned down at her. "Well, until tonight, that is, and we see how well that one worked out."

She returned the grin. "Welcome to my world, pal. The last date I had before Vin was a guy from a dating site. He was an ass, but that only slightly lessened the sting of him saying that he thought I'd be smaller. I walked out on him and that was the best date I'd had in almost two years."

Sean shook his head as if to clear it. "He said that? He thought you'd be *smaller*? Seriously?"

Megan raised her hand and gave him a thumbs-up. "Right to my face. You see, he really only dates women who are size six or smaller. Sometimes an eight if they're tall and can pull it off."

"Oh. My. God. What a douche!" Sean was clearly flummoxed and Meg cherished that about him.

She had no idea what Sean Flaherty thought about her body—that wasn't a part of their relationship, nor had it ever really been. At least not since they'd gotten out of high school. For a brief time in junior year, she'd harbored a small crush on him, pretty much like every other girl in their class. When he'd stepped in and taken her to the Christmas formal after Karl Schwimmer had dumped her three days before because Ashley Boggs crooked her little finger at him, Megan had almost fallen in love with Sean. Dancing in the arms of the star basketball player, student body president, and hottest guy in the class had been sheer heaven. Meg had basked in the envious glances from her friends that night.

But after the dance, he'd kept her strictly in the friend zone, while he focused on stealing Ashley from Karl in a game of one-upmanship that had started freshman year and carried on right through graduation. Somehow staying just friends with the great Sean Flaherty seemed simpler and they'd fallen back in their old camaraderie.

Not that she didn't notice how strong and handsome he was, she did. She'd have to be blind not to; but now she noticed in the same way she appreciated a fine piece of art or a good-looking actor or movie star. There was nothing more than friendship between the two of them, so when he reached out and stroked one long finger down her cheek, the wave of longing that swept through her startled her.

When he tunneled his fingers under her hair and leaned over to touch his forehead to hers, her heart pounded.

"Megan Mackenzie, you are a beautiful, luscious woman. Don't ever let anyone tell you different." His voice was husky and his eyes turned navy blue with emotion.

Their gazes locked for a long moment.

I should move away.

The thought had no more flitted through her mind before Sean's lips touched hers—just the lightest kiss, but it stole her breath away. Then he canted his head and took her mouth with a hunger that shocked her all the way to her toes.

Chapter Ten

THE YEARNING THAT had been building in her over-flowed. Megan slid her hands up Sean's chest and put her arms around his neck, thrusting her fingers in the thick dark hair that grew over his collar. She returned the kiss with a fervor that stunned her, opening her lips to his insistent mouth, basking in the wine-sweet warmth of their mingled breath. He took her lips again and again and she was right there with him meeting him kiss for ravenous kiss.

Desire pooled in her belly, so intense it filled the space between them almost like something material that she could touch, and she wanted more. Needed more. More of his lips. More of his hands on her. More... She met his seeking tongue with her own, tasting Donal's port, as she skimmed her hand down his bicep, caressing the muscles that had grown even firmer from all the PT he'd been doing.

He drew her closer, breaking the contact with her mouth to kiss a path across her cheek and then touch his tongue to her ear before capturing her lips once more. When he moaned and slid his other hand down to her hip, tugging her almost onto his lap, reality smacked her in the head.

This is Sean!

Wrenching herself from his arms, she leaped up and nearly tripped over the trunk in front of them, knocking over the small stemmed glass of port she'd set there earlier. She couldn't catch her breath as she stared in horror at the dark purple stain spreading across the top of the lake-blue-painted trunk. She grabbed the first thing she could find to keep the liquid from running onto the seagrass rug. Her sweater. The new white pima cotton sweater she'd just paid fifty-two dollars and thirty-three cents for including tax and shipping.

With tears stinging her eyes, she uttered an oath in French that her mother would be both horrified and amused to hear come out of her daughter's mouth, and gathered the sweater in both hands, along with a wet magazine and three soggy crocheted coasters.

Sean sat on the settee, looking pie-eyed.

She glared at him. "Are you going to help me clean this up... or no?"

"What's *fils de pute?*" He pronounced the curse with an appalling French accent as lust and confusion glowed in his blue eyes... and he still hadn't moved. He just sat there, his hands folded in his lap. "I know *merde*—I've heard you say that one often enough, so what's *fils de pute?*"

For half a second, she wanted to hurl the whole mess into his lap, shove his sore leg off the trunk, and storm out, but his expression was so peculiar, it stopped her. "What is it? Are you okay?" When he didn't respond right away, she persisted. "Are you hurting?"

Sean closed his eyes and dropped his head back, then raised it again and this time something that looked like a cross between frustration and... *wait, is that glee?* shone on his too-handsome face. "I'm fine." His straight white teeth caught his lower lip. "Um. I just... I just need to sit here for a minute or two."

Dear Lord, what was the matter with him?

Suddenly, it struck her like a thunderbolt why he wasn't moving, why his hands were covering... *oh, holy...* Heat rose from her neck to her cheeks, but she couldn't make herself look away from him, from his lap.

He raised one dark brow when he caught her staring, lifted his hands, looked down, and then back up at her with rueful smile. "Aye, and who knew, after all these years, you could have *this* kind of effect on me, Meggy Mackenzie." The Irish lilt that always came out when he was particularly stressed turned the words into a caress.

For a brief second, she willed the floor to open up so she could fall into a deep dark hole and the whole nightmare evening would be over. "Sean, I-I... I'm..." Chagrined, she couldn't seem to form an intelligent sentence. She simply stood there gaping at him, her hands sticky from the wine soaked into her sweater and her face hot with embarrassment. Her lips trembled and she blinked furiously to keep from completing her humiliation by bursting into tears.

Sean *umphed* himself up from the settee, got his balance

with his cane, and with the other hand, swept the mess from her fingers and carried it to the kitchen sink. Dumping it all into one side, he yanked the magazine out and dropped it into the trash can beside the bar. He flipped the faucet on, letting cold water run over her sweater and the coasters as he washed his hands. "Meg, come here." He crooked his finger at her.

His grin was the old Sean—the one who could charm her into doing his math homework because even though Sean Flaherty was the star of the debate team, he sucked at sophomore algebra. Hesitating, she finally crossed to the kitchen and put her hands under the cold water to rinse off the wine, staring in disgust at what she'd done to her new sweater.

He offered her a towel, tilting his head toward the sink. "Well, I think that one's a goner."

Ignoring the towel, she pulled a length of paper towels from the roll above the sink, wet it, and went into the porch to try to rescue the wicker trunk. By some miracle, she'd gotten all the wine off the top of the thing with her sweater, and even when she opened it, there was no sign of any port having leaked through onto the blankets inside. She was running the towels over the lid anyway when she felt his presence behind her.

"Hey, it's fine." He took the clump of paper towels from her and hurled it into the kitchen, where it hit the granite countertop with a *splat*. "Stop." Tossing the cane on the settee, he grasped her shoulders in his big hands. "Stop now, Meggy, talk to me."

THEY WERE STANDING so close Sean could feel the heat of her blush radiating off her cheeks and even that set his heart to pounding. He breathed deeply, inhaling the familiar and yet somehow brand-new scent of Megan Mackenzie.

"What would you like me to say, Sean?" Megan wasn't looking at him.

Instead her glance darted around the room, making her appear like a frightened doe. She grabbed the tea towel he'd tossed over his shoulder, just like Da always did when he cooked or was working in the wine cellar. After drying her hands briskly, she shoved the scrap of terry cloth at him as she twisted out of his grasp and stepped around him.

"I think I've pretty much reached my humiliation tolerance for one night, so... see ya." Before he could catch his breath, her footsteps clicked on the hardwood floor of the foyer.

Geez, that woman moved fast... and he couldn't, *dammit*.

"Megan, wait!" Sean hopped on his left leg, trying to get turned around in the narrow space between the settee and the trunk without falling over. She was gone, the front door shut softly behind her. He hobbled to the door and yanked it open just in time to see her backing out of the driveway.

Damn. Damn. Damn.

He sagged against the doorjamb, watching the little Honda's red taillights disappear in a cloud of gravel dust. Suddenly, he was exhausted. When he shut the door, he stopped for a moment to rest, leaning back on the heavy wood. His right leg ached, as did other parts southward— something that both delighted and astonished him. How long had it been since... he tried to recall the last time that kind of desire had hit him with such force and he couldn't. He flexed his fingers, remembering Meg's soft skin, how she'd shivered when he kissed her, and the hunger that hadn't yet fully subsided grew inside him again.

He wanted her. He wanted his best friend.

It was that simple... and that complicated.

He took a deep breath. If they continued on this road, there was no returning to just friends, not ever. He chewed his lower lip, his lust-fogged brain going back to Megan's lush mouth opening to his, the little groan that escaped when he touched her ear with his tongue, the scent of her hair... How could he go back after tasting her kisses, experiencing the bliss of holding her in his arms?

Straightening, he limped to the kitchen, pulled out the little crocheted coasters, and tossed them in the trash. *Sorry, Char.* He gently wrung out the white-turning-purple sweater and carried it to the small laundry room between the kitchen and the garage. The sweater looked like cotton, so maybe he could rescue it. Holding it above the laundry tub, he read the label. Yup, it was cotton, so he ran about an inch or two of water into the deep sink and dropped it in. If memory served, Da's answer to wine stains was a mixture of three parts hydrogen peroxide and one part of that blue dish soap.

With a smile, he shook his head. Sure enough, the bottles were front and center in the cupboard above the washing machine and the recipe for wine stain removal—in Da's blocky script—was taped to the inside of the door. He grabbed the cup measure, mixed up the solution, and added it to the water, pressing to make sure the sweater was fully submerged. Twenty minutes ought to do it. While he was waiting, he'd sit down with his iPad, find the company from the label inside the cardigan, and order her a new one.

Half an hour later, he settled onto the sofa and started undoing the brace around his thigh. The mostly white sweater was in the washing machine with some bleach and detergent, a new one was on its way to Meg's office on the second floor of the town hall, and his head was still full of her lush curves and blond curls. Her peachy skin and tanned legs. And those eyes... Brown was a weak description. *Brandy* was better. Huge and expressive, they sparkled with copper-colored light when she laughed, but turned dark when she was upset or emotional. Tonight they'd been the color of rich cognac...

His phone vibrated against his leg and he practically tore the button off his shorts pocket getting the thing out, hoping it was a text from Megan.

It was from Vin. *"I'm on your porch. Open the door."*

"Why should I?" Sean thumbed back.

"Just do it."

With a sigh, he removed the brace, heaved himself off the couch, and grabbed his cane. When he opened the door, there was Vin, somehow looking contrite and cocky all at the same time. An expression Sean had seen more times than he could count. The anger that had been simmering in him since he and Meg had walked out of the diner boiled over and without a second thought, he threw a punch that hit Vin squarely in the jaw and sent him sprawling on the wood floor of the porch.

Holding his cheek, Vin managed to get awkwardly to his feet.

He moved his jawbone around gingerly before he spoke. "You know, that bad-ass scar on your leg is the only thing keeping me from beating the hell out of you right now." He rubbed his mouth and then looked at his hand.

Sean was only sorry that Vin didn't find teeth in his palm… or at least a little blood. "Admit it, Vin, you deserved that." Under cover of darkness, he massaged his knuckles. He hadn't hit anyone since junior high. Damn, it made his hand sore.

"What did I do?" Vin whined and turned, spitting over the porch rail before coming back into the pool of light from the two coach lights on either side of the door.

Sean rested his good shoulder against the doorjamb to

get some of the weight off his bad leg. "The fact that you even have to ask should shock me, but somehow after all these years of watching you play the victim, it doesn't."

Vin crossed his arms over his chest and snorted an indignant laugh. "*She* walked out on *me*, man, and by the way, it was freaking rude of you to just leave poor Gia all alone like—"

Sean huffed an exasperated breath. "Don't even go there, Vin. She wasn't alone. She was with *you*."

"You just can't stand it, can you?" Vin backed away and leaned on the porch rail, his old supercilious façade back in place.

"What the hell are you talking about?" Sean was tired and frustrated and struggling to keep from kicking the bastard down the steps and being done with it.

"It burns your butt that the ladies prefer me," Vin said with a smug grin that Sean wanted to wipe off his face with his cane. "It always has."

The inanity of that statement, along with Vin's utter lack of understanding of his own culpability in the disastrous evening, suddenly struck Sean as hilarious and he chuckled. In seconds, the chuckle turned into full-on laughter and he chortled as Vin straightened, his bruised chin stuck out in defiance.

"Admit it, Flaherty," he said, keeping at least a cane's length away.

"Push off, Vinnie." Sean shook his head. "Go back to

Chicago. And don't ever contact Megan Mackenzie again, because if you do, I swear—"

"Oh, my God!" Now Vin was the one chortling. "Oh, my God, *you're* in love with her!"

Sean's gut tightened at the stark truth of Vin's words, but that wasn't a hill he was willing to climb right now, especially not with Vinnie DeLuca. "Just go." He pushed off the doorjamb and leaning on his cane, backed inside. "I'm serious, Vin. Stay away from Megan."

He shut the door and leaned his forehead against it, eyes closed.

"He's right, you know."

He spun around at Char's soft words. There she stood in her long pink robe, her gray-blond hair awry. He'd never even heard her come into the foyer. When she didn't come down to greet them earlier, he assumed she was in bed since she had a seven A.M. flight to Florida the next day. Their eyes met and she half-hitched one shoulder. "Honey, it's been plain as day ever since you came home—the two of you are moving toward something new. Maybe it's time for you to decide what you're going to do about Megan Mackenzie."

Chapter Eleven

"WHAT HAPPENED TO you, kid?"

Her father gazed at her as Megan poured herself a cup of coffee, doctored it with half-and-half and a packet of sweetener, then dropped onto the end stool at the Riverside. She sipped, grateful for the warmth that spread through her because she had been unnaturally chilled for the last forty-eight hours. It was July in Indiana for Pete's sake. The last thing she should've been was cold.

A bran muffin appeared on a plate in front of her and when she looked up, Mac was leaning against the back counter still staring intently at her, his brawny arms crossed over his chest.

"You gonna talk?" He raised one brow. "'cause you look like something the cat dragged in."

"I'm okay." She took another drink of the soothing liquid, but the muffin didn't look even a little bit appetizing.

"No, you're not. You've been incommunicado since Friday night. You didn't show up for supper last night. Some lame text excuse about having a headache—"

"I *had* a headache, Dad."

"That's never kept you from Sunday night dinner before."

"I'm here now." Megan hoped her terse replies would send the message that she wasn't in the mood for a heart-to-heart. "And I'm okay."

Mac glanced at his watch. "It's six in the morning. I'm not even open yet. It's clear you haven't slept in at least one night, possibly two, plus you're in a hoodie, even though it's already seventy-five degrees outside. So, start talking... or do I make a call to Paris, where it's currently noon and your mother is probably on a shoot?"

"Are you seriously threatening to call *Mère*?" Megan met his probing eyes. "Just because I didn't come to dinner last night? Dad, I'm thirty-seven years old." Her father sometimes forgot that she wasn't the little girl he'd brought home with him from France. His and Mère's divorce had been quite amicable, even when he asked to take eleven-year-old Meg back to the States with him. Mère had agreed, knowing her high-powered career in the world of fashion would mean nannies or boarding school. However, frequent trips to Paris each year kept the mother-daughter bond strong and gave Megan a chance to experience the world, which her dad supported fully.

"Nope." Mac uncrossed his arms and leaned over her to drop a kiss on her forehead. "I'm threatening to call your mom because something's happened and you won't talk to *me*." He zipped to the end of the counter, vaulted the swinging gate—something she'd seen him do at least ten thousand times in her life—and plopped onto the stool next to her. "I've got bacon in the oven and I have to unlock that door in less than thirty minutes, so give. What happened with the cop this weekend? Do I need to break out my shotgun?"

In spite of her bad humor, Megan giggled. "You don't own a shotgun, Papa."

He jerked a thumb north. "There's a Walmart up on the highway. I can own a shotgun in twenty minutes. Do I need one?"

"No." She shook her head. "It just didn't work out."

"Do you want to expand on that?" Mac rose and stood behind her to rub her shoulders and, dear God, he knew exactly where to find the knots and kinks. He always had, ever since she was a little girl.

"Not really, but thanks."

He pressed his thumbs into the hollows where her neck and shoulders met, gently easing the tension. "The right guy is out there, baby."

Megan snorted, then lied through her teeth. "I'm just fine without a man. As a matter of fact, I'm beginning to wonder if I need to get another cat... or two. Maybe a kitten. Janet's cat, Fiona, just had kittens. I saw them when I went into the Yarn Basket last week. They were cute. I can totally pull off crazy cat lady, don't you think?"

Except she wasn't fine at all. Nor did she want a kitten.

What she *did* want was a man—Sean Flaherty, to be precise. Holy Pete, what a freakin' mess she was.

"Come on, it's not that bad." He spun her around on the stool to face him. "Besides, I don't imagine Mamie Eisenhower would take kindly to a kitten invading her territory. She's got you all trained."

Megan blinked. By God, she wasn't going to break down again—not after spending all of Saturday and Sunday alternately crying and shivering at the thought of Sean Flaherty's kisses. How could something that felt so incredibly right in the moment seem so very wrong this morning?

However, Sean wasn't who her dad was referring to, and Friday night wasn't something she was prepared to discuss with anyone just yet. Not her beloved father or even Sam, although her new bestie would be coming around for details soon enough. She was certain the only thing keeping Sam at bay at this point was the fear that she'd interrupt whatever *affaire de coeur*, as Mère would call it, that might have been going on between Meg and that snake, Vinnie DeLuca.

Megan had deliberately *not* phoned Sam all weekend, content to let her believe that she and Vin were holed up in her apartment doing all the stuff Megan had fantasized about for weeks. She was too confused, too baffled to try to talk it all out. She had to sort it out in her own head first. Thing was, she wasn't sorting anything at all; she was still fantasizing, except it wasn't Vinnie's whose kisses and touches she was imagining. It was Sean's. However, he'd been mysteriously quiet all weekend, too. Probably beating himself up for what had happened. The thought made her throat tighten.

She rose, grabbed the muffin, wrapped it in a napkin, and pecked her dad on his bristly cheek. "I love you, Papa."

Mac stopped her with a hand on her shoulder. "Then let me make you some eggs."

"Thanks, but no. I'm going to go take a brisk bike ride along the river and then go home, eat this muffin, shower, and get ready for work. I've got a council meeting tonight and I need to prepare for it." She gave him the most convincing smile she could muster. "I'm good, I promise, and I'll be back this afternoon because Sam and I are coming in for iced tea and pie. I'll see you later."

"Con? Hey, where are you?" Sean shouldered the downstairs door to the winery open, peering into the hallway. He followed the sound of someone cursing and banging on metal to the high-ceilinged room that held six huge stainless-steel fermentation tanks, as well as several rows of oak barrels. "Con?" He raised his volume a notch higher, hoping he wouldn't have to tramp around every tank to find his brother.

Scowling and sweating, Conor appeared from behind one of the tanks. "I'm here."

"What's up?" Sean made his way across the damp concrete floor.

"Freakin' racking valve on number three is stuck again and the tank's leaking." Conor smacked the offending tank. "Da wanted to get rid of this white elephant three years ago. He was talking about it the morning"—he shook his head—"the morning he died."

"Well, why don't we replace it?"

Conor tossed the hammer on a wooden keg and yanked off his gloves. "Thirteen grand? Not right now. Not after the fortune we just spent on the new roof for the tasting room in town. We gotta wait until after the first of the year. See how we do with these summer pizza-and-wine nights and over the holidays." He brightened. "Want to taste the zin? The Dry Creek grapes were unbelievable—worth every penny—and it's the first red that Da left entirely to me. It's about ready to bottle." He grabbed a wine thief and a glass from a nearby rack that held newly sterilized equipment.

"Sure." Sean bit back his first reaction, which was to suggest Conor accept the money that Aidan had offered only last month to replace two old fermenters and buy more French oak barrels. Conor had refused with, *Thanks, bro, but would Da have taken your money?* Aidan had to admit their father had always refused to accept any help from his very successful sons, insisting the winery had to make its own way.

On the other hand…

As Sean followed his brother's long stride to the third

row of barrels, he debated reminding Conor that Aidan had a stake in Four Irish Brothers Winery now, too, and maybe putting some of the fortune their kid brother had made starring in a television series into the winery would be a good idea.

As Conor used the wine thief to draw zinfandel from one of the oak barrels, Sean jumped in with both feet. "Con, two new fermentation tanks and some oak barrels would be nothing to Aidan's bank account, and you'd make him pretty happy if he could invest some of that wicked LA money here."

Conor handed him the tasting glass of wine. "Here, try this. See if you think it needs to be racked again."

Sean accepted the small tumbler, watching as Conor drew another couple of ounces from the barrel and made his own glass of zinfandel. "It's not the same, Conor. When Aidan tried to help before, this place belonged to Da. He let his pride keep him from taking money from his son, even though he was the one who kept telling us that Four Irish Brothers was a *family* winery. Now it's *ours*. We're all four equal partners."

Conor eyed him, one dark brow raised. "Taste the wine, Sean."

Sean held the glass up to the sunlight, then swirled it, watching the wine's "legs" slide down the side of the tumbler. Before he drank, he tried again. "You've been great about talking to us about the wines and about what you're doing here. You have Meg send those quarterly reports like clockwork, but it's like you're reporting in to a board of directors or something."

Conor glanced at him, took a sip of wine, and swished it for a moment, obviously letting it touch all his taste buds. He held the wine in his mouth a second or two longer, his eyes closed, and his lips turned up in the slightest smile.

In that moment, he looked so much like Da, Sean's heart wrenched. "Conor…"

His little brother opened his eyes and spat on the floor near the drain. "Please, just taste the damn wine."

Sean sighed and sniffed the glass. The aromas of jam and oak and spice were immediately evident; however, none overpowered. His mouth watered. He sipped, swishing the liquid around on his tongue as berries and spice filled his sense. The flavor was so rich and complex, he couldn't bring himself to spit, so he swallowed the wine, then gazed at his brother, the winemaker. "Oh, my God, Conor. This… this is amazing. You've gone beyond Da's zin to"—he couldn't find the words, so he just shook his head—"honestly, when this is ready to go into the bottle, it's going to rival anything we've ever tasted in California."

Conor grinned. "It's the grapes. After I set up a college fund for Ali, I used the rest of the insurance money from Emmy to buy the best grapes I could get from Dry Creek. I went out and chose them from the vineyard, instead of just ordering whatever we could get like Da always did. They survived the trip, thank heavens. He thought I was crazy to spend so much, but... Wow, huh? I don't think we need to rack it again. Da probably would, but I don't think it's over-oaked, do you?"

"I think it's great just like it is. We should get it into the bottles soon." Sean held his glass up to toast, Conor clinked with him, and they both drank. Conor even swallowed this time after savoring the delicious flavors.

"Do you have a name for it yet?" Sean set his empty glass on the closest wine barrel. "Maybe we should name it after Emmy, or would it be too weird to name a wine after your deceased wife?"

Conor gave him a half-smile. "It would be too weird. I... I don't think I can put her actual name on it, but I'd like to honor her. I was talking to Sam about it and she suggested Teacher's Pet Zin, since Em was a teacher."

"I like it. It's perfect." He opened his mouth to speak, closed it, then went ahead with it. "Conny, come on, take the money from Aidan and buy the new tanks. You make incredible wine. Don't let your stupid pride keep you from doing that." Sean nodded, then reached out and ruffled Conor's already-tousled hair. "Let us in, man. We want to be a part in any way we can."

Conor stared at him, his blue eyes shimmering.

He sucked in a deep breath and released it slowly. "I'll think about it."

Sean nodded and his "good laddie" offered in Da's broad

brogue brought a chuckle and a little mistiness from both of them.

After a quick bro-hug, Sean pointed to the door. "I'm actually here for wine. I'm headed into town to fill the racks. We had good traffic over the weekend and we're low on almost everything. I've got the bank deposit ready, too, so if you have yours, I'll run by and do the banking on my way."

"That'd be great, thanks. Mine's upstairs, I'll grab it before you leave. Is Char's Tahoe outside?" At Sean's nod, Conor lifted his chin toward the storeroom. "Okay, let's load you up."

They both carried cases of wine with Sean moving a bit slower than Conor, even though he was walking pretty well without the cane—something that Conor noted when they shoved the last box into the back of the car.

"I'm getting there." Sean swiped his forearm across his sweating brow. "I still need the walking stick if I'm going any distance or it's late in the day, so I keep it close. I've decided it makes me look dashing, so I may just hang on to it."

Conor chuckled. "A real chick magnet, huh?" He snapped his fingers. "Oh, hey, speaking of chick magnets, how'd it go with Gia on Friday night? Things were so nuts here and you were in town all weekend, so I haven't had a chance to ask you about it."

Sean leaned against the back of the Tahoe. "It didn't."

"No spark?"

"Oh, there was a spark all right"—Sean snorted a grim

laugh—"between Vinnie and Gia."

Conor's eyes widened. "Oh, holy hell. No wonder I didn't see Meg and Vinnie at pizza-and-wine night on Saturday. I half thought the two of them were, you know, hanging out at her place." He air-quoted the last few words.

Sean's gut tightened at the clear message in those words and he was even gladder than ever that he'd punched Vin Friday night. The thought of that guy's hands on Megan sent a cold chill through him. Truth be told, the thought of anyone's hands except his touching her made him see red. He sat on the back of the open SUV and gazed out across the vineyard, breathing in the warm, scented air, remembering Meg's soft skin, her hair tumbling over her shoulders, her delicious lips.

As Conor shoved the last case into the car, he eyed Sean curiously. "How was Meg about it? I hope she told him to…" He lifted his chin in the general direction of north.

Sean smiled. "Oh, yeah, she scorched him—right there in the middle of al fresco dining at Mac's. The place was packed. It was a beautiful thing to see."

Conor leaned one shoulder against the SUV. "I never realized what a true douche that guy is."

"It was his usual MO. He's never met a woman he could resist."

"Poor Megs. She deserves better."

"She's going to be fine. I'll make sure of it." Sean rubbed a hand over his weekend stubble, noting Conor's sudden curious glance. "Con, I…" He searched for the right words. The time he'd spent over the weekend running the in-town tasting room, pouring tastings, chatting with customers as he served them wine and cheese on the deck that overlooked the Ohio River, even helping Gracie and Chris, their two weekend employees, clean up and close was the best time he'd had in years. And then there was Megan…

"What's the matter, dude?" Conor peered down at him, concern showing in his blue eyes that were almost an exact match of Sean's own.

Sean bit the inside of his cheek, unsure what would happen if he finally said aloud the words he'd been thinking for the past few weeks.

"I don't want to go back to Chicago."

Chapter Twelve

SEAN SWALLOWED HARD, watching a parade of reactions cross his brother's face—astonishment, delight, curiosity—but fortunately, no sign of dismay.

"Shove over." Conor plopped down on the back of the SUV next to him. "What's this all about? I'd have thought you'd be more than ready to get back to your big-city life." He held up one hand. "Right off though, let me say I'd like nothing more than for you to move back here and be a part of this place."

Sean shoulder-nudged him. "Thanks, Conny. This may sound crazy, but ever since I made partner, it's seemed as though there's never an hour for *me*. I'm always at the office or in court or attending meetings. I don't have a single moment to call my own."

"I didn't realize. I've always assumed you were doing what you love."

"I do love… well, I *did* love being a lawyer. At first, it was exciting and rewarding, especially when I could help save a marriage." He chuckled grimly. "Lately, I haven't had the best track record on that front, and, God Almighty, there's so freakin' much acrimony. Hell, look at what happened when I helped Kent Grey win custody of his kids from his junkie wife." He pointed to his healing thigh. "How can two people who promised to love each other forever suddenly hate each other? Hate each other so much they want to commit murder? Because, by God, she was out to kill both of us. How does that happen?"

Conor's shoulders rose and he smiled. "You're talking to a guy who married his childhood sweetheart, lost her, and then fell in love at first sight, ass over elbows, as Da always said, with his current fiancée. I got no clue how marriages go south."

Sean nodded. "I know. Being around you and Sam reminds me of Da and Ma. How happy they were together. I'm so glad for you, I am…" He ransacked his mind for the right words to describe the emptiness that had been inside his soul for months—even before the shooting. "Remember at New Year's, when I offered Sam a sabbatical from the firm?"

Conor nodded. "And she said no and resigned instead. Sorry, not sorry, dude."

"I was so jealous I could hardly see straight." Sean pressed his lips together and swallowed hard. "I'm happy for you and Sam, and I'm also envious as hell. I need some happy in my life, Con. I want to wake up *not* dreading what the new day has in store. This"—he touched the brace on his thigh that showed below the hem of his shorts—"has made me reassess everything. I want a life, a real life."

"Your life in Chicago isn't real?"

Sean smirked. "It's too real."

"How hard would it be for you to leave the firm since you're a partner?"

"I've got the *title* of partner, but even though my name's part of the banner, I'm not an *equity partner* yet. I'm too new, so there's no buyout involved. I could give them notice, leave, and take my 401K with me. Charlie wants to make me a part-owner sooner than was originally planned because of the shooting. Turns out nearly getting killed impressed the profit-sharing partners so much, they'd like to bring me *into the fold* as Charlie puts it. My buy-in would be a shot of cash to the firm, not that they need it." Sean shook his head. "The one thing I thought I wanted more than anything, something I believed wouldn't happen for another five years at least? Now the very thought of it makes my gut ache."

Conor's eyes grew wider. "Sean, that's huge. You've been working your ass off up there. You've earned this."

Sean shrugged. "Maybe I have earned it, but not by getting shot up by some client's crazy ex." He rose, paced a few slow steps up the drive, and then turned back to the SUV. "And I don't think it's what I want more than anything in the world anymore."

"You'd better be damn sure you don't want it before you toss away a twelve-year, hard-fought career." Conor's words echoed Sean's own chaotic feelings. "Could you be truly happy here, taking care of the vineyard and working with me? I'd love it if you stayed. It's been awesome having you back home, but how much would it suck if you gave up big-city lawyering, and realized it was a mistake?" He grinned. "It gets awfully quiet here come January."

"That sounds like heaven to me." Sean returned to the car and ruffled Conor's dark hair, noting, apropos of nothing at all, that they both needed haircuts. His own hair was growing over his ears and curling on his neck in the back. Funny, he hadn't even noticed 'til now.

In Chicago, he got his hair trimmed every two weeks—a standing Saturday morning appointment at the shop in the lobby of the building that housed the firm. Truth be told, he had no idea how much that haircut cost because he simply signed a voucher that got paid by the firm before folding a hefty cash tip into Ron, the barber's, hand as he walked out the door. That was how all the partners did it. Then back to work. Saturdays, even Sundays, hunched over his desk in the office was his usual weekend routine.

He shook his head in bewilderment. What did it say about him that he didn't know how much his haircuts cost? "I'm going up next Tuesday to meet with Charlie and the other partners. If I do this, there's no going back, and frankly, several guys behind me would love to help me pack, so I've got to be really sure."

"Can I ask you a question?" Hesitation colored Conor's tone.

"Of course."

"Are you *scared* to go back? I mean did that"—he nodded toward Sean's thigh—"make you want to leave the city?"

Sean stroked his jaw, then slid his hand around to rub the back of his neck. "It's probably part of it. According to the therapist, it wouldn't be unusual. I keep thinking I should go back just to prove I can."

"Prove to whom?" Conor's question was pure Donal Flaherty and Sean was struck again at how very much his little brother was like Da. "You don't have anything to prove, Sean. Nobody would blame you if you never stepped foot in a courtroom again."

"Maybe..." Sean chewed his lower lip. There was more to his wanting to move back, but he wasn't sure he was ready to reveal what had happened with Megan on Char's screened porch. The memory of that time was still too fresh; he needed to process it and more important, he had to talk to Megan.

On the other hand, how would he ever know if what he was feeling for her—this unfamiliar ache that started deep in his chest and ended up someplace farther south as he imagined touching her soft skin, kissing her luscious lips—was real or only another reaction to being shot and coming home? "Can I ask you a question?" He repeated Conor's words from a moment ago.

Conor's eyes sparkled with curiosity. "Of course, ask me anything."

"How did you know Sam was the one? I mean after Emmy… did you think you'd ever love anyone again… you know… like you did her?" Sean faltered over the words, mentally cursing his tripping tongue. *Dammit.* He sounded like a teenager. "Did it happen gradually or did it hit you between the eyes?"

Conor grinned. "Sam knocked my socks off from the moment I first saw her all wet and frustrated, cursing at the spare on her Beemer. Why?"

Sean shrugged. "Just curious."

"Is there someone?" Conor rose and peered at him with a look that seemed to see inside him—Da's probing expression. "Someone in Chicago?"

"No. There's no one."

A muscle worked in Conor's jaw as he gazed at Sean. "For what it's worth, it was different with Em, although I thought she was beautiful the first time I saw her way back in eighth grade. We grew up together and that was a nice way to fall in love, too."

Sean offered him a small smile. "You still have faith in childhood sweethearts?"

"I do. Absolutely." Conor eyed him for a few seconds. "I even have faith in childhood *friends* who might one day realize they're in love."

Sean's breath caught in his throat and he turned away, taking several steps toward the front of the Tahoe. When he looked over his shoulder, Conor was right behind him, his arms crossed over his chest, a knowing smile on his face.

"Do you think I'm blind, you big idiot?"

Sean dug in his shorts pocket for the keys. "I have no idea what you're talking about." The words came out shaky.

"I think you do." Conor put one hand on the driver's door handle, stopping Sean from opening it. "You're in love with your best friend and I'm not talking about Vinnie. You shout it to the world every time you look at Megan. Now the question is, what are you going to do about it?"

Hadn't Char asked him that very same question only three nights ago?

Sean dropped back against the side of the car, suddenly needing to take some weight off his healing leg. He ran his hands over his face again and then raked his fingers through his hair.

There was no point in denying the accusation, so he opted for honesty. "I have no freakin' idea." Straightening, he limped the two feet to the driver's seat and slid into the Tahoe. His leg ached. "I gotta get going. Chris is meeting me to rack wine bottles, the deck needs to be hosed down, and the guy from Sycamore Hills is delivering cheese and sausage this afternoon. I'll bring you yours after I get done."

"You gonna be okay?" Conor closed the door as Sean started the engine and hit the button to roll down the window. "I can come down and help you. Sam and I refilled racks here last night after we closed."

"I've got Chris. I'm good."

"I stuck the bank deposit on the seat there." Conor peered into the car, squinting against the sunlight streaming in the other side of the SUV.

"I saw." Sean glanced at the passenger seat where two bank bags lay atop a large pizza box. "Oh, and thanks for the leftover pizza. Looks like breakfast to me. Chris'll be thrilled."

Grinning, Conor stepped away, then put a hand on the door again. "You know, there are lots of good reasons to turn your life upside down. In my opinion, love's one of the best. If you don't believe me, just ask Sam."

"CAN WE WALK?" Megan met Sam on the sidewalk as she came out of the old Victorian that housed the law offices of Harold Evans, Esq.

"No pie?" Sam raised one brow. "It's key lime today. I ran into Paula this morning when I grabbed coffee at your dad's."

"I'll text Dad and tell him to save you a piece. We need to talk." Megan headed toward the River Walk, glancing over her shoulder to make sure Sam was right behind her.

"Is this about Vin? How'd it go?" Sam caught up. "I wanted to call you, but I didn't want to… you know… interrupt anything."

"It's not about Vin… Well, it is, but it isn't." Megan

increased her stride, taking the path along the mighty Ohio at a brisk pace as she attempted to put her scattered thoughts into enough of a story to tell Sam.

"Meg, slow down!" Sam race-walked to keep up. "Lord, what's up with you today? What happened?"

Meg stopped in the middle of the path and turned around. "Sean and I kissed."

Sam, who'd practically walked past her when she'd halted so suddenly, backed up a step or two, gazing at Megan in a look of astonishment that turned to a frown. "Damn," she said finally. "I owe Conor a buck."

Megan scowled. *"What?"*

"Oh, we had a bet. He's been telling me since Sean got home there was something going on between the two of you and I told him he was crazy." Sam jerked her head toward the path. "Come on, let's walk and you can tell me everything."

Megan, too floored to even take a step, stood still as Sam walked on. Had Sean said something to Conor about her? Were the two of them a hot topic among the Flaherty brothers all of a sudden?

"Are you coming or not?" Sam hollered from a couple hundred feet ahead. "I want details."

Megan shook her head and caught up to Sam. "Why does Conor think there's something more than friendship between me and Sean?"

Sam shrugged. "He says you two are sending off *a vibe.*"

She air-quoted. "Maybe it's a brother thing. Those four are scary connected sometimes."

Megan's heart rose to her throat, then fell to her socks, and then came back to her throat again as she remembered Sean's hands on her, his fingers tangling in her hair as he'd kissed her. Kisses like she'd never experienced before—hot and passionate and yet so full of tenderness she'd wanted to crawl inside his heart and stay there forever.

But it was *Sean*.

And, okay, there *was* a vibe. She'd be lying if she denied it, so she didn't even try. Instead she started at the beginning as she and Sam walked the path through the trees along the river, pouring out the entire story of the disastrous date with Vin and the startling, yet somehow not, moments on Char's screened porch with Sean later.

"I can't believe Gia did that." Sam huffed, her arms pumping as they sped around the circle at the east end of the River Walk and began retracing their steps. "Can we slow down, please? I've got a client coming in at two and I don't have time to take another shower. As it is, I'm going to have to go upstairs and do a quick bird bath when we get back. After I slap Gia around. Sheesh."

Megan shortened her stride, swiping a hand over the curls plastered against her cheek. "Don't bother. I don't blame Gia. You've seen Vin. He's gorgeous and irresistible. I hope they had a lovely weekend together." She blew a long breath up into her bangs. "Funny, I don't even blame *him*

143

anymore. But, Sam..." She gave her friend a pleading look. "What am I going to do about Sean?"

"Personally, I'd explore it. What have you got to lose?" Sam slowed her steps even more as they approached the street that led back up to her law office and the town square.

"How about over twenty years of friendship?" Megan trudged up the gentle hill that was Adams Street. "What if all he needs is a... a wubbie."

"A *what?*" Sam chuckled and wiped her brow with a tissue. "What's a wubbie?"

"You know, like a security blanket? He's right off a terrifying experience. He's back home healing among family and friends. Life is safe here. *I'm* safe. What if that's all it is?" Megan's throat constricted at the thought because, truth was, she was aching for Sean Flaherty. The night before, in a rare moment of self-discovery that had occurred as she'd been gazing unseeing at the town budget, she'd realized Sean had always been the high-water mark for her dating life. All the men she'd gone out with over the years and none of them had ever measured up to her best friend.

Eyes stinging, she stopped at the top of the hill and turned to Sam. "I don't want to be *safe.*"

Chapter Thirteen

MEGAN GAZED OUT at the group of River's Edge citizens who had come to the emergency town meeting she'd called, but the person she'd most hoped to see wasn't in the crowd. She sighed and watched as her assistant scurried around a long table set with a checked tablecloth, loaded with trays of Paula Meadows's cookies and two huge vats of icy cold lemonade. Stepping across the impromptu stage that had been put up on the grass across from the River Walk, she shook herself and focused on the task at hand—calling the citizens to order. It was time to unveil the plan she'd been working on for most of her term as mayor.

Over her shoulder was the old Parrish cotton mill. The historic structure, which was the best remaining example of nineteenth-century industry on the riverfront, had been abandoned when the mill ceased production back in the late nineteen eighties. Built in eighteen seventy-four, it had served the town well for over a hundred years, providing jobs and security, but now with its broken windows and crumbling façade, it was an eyesore. The last owner had died several years ago and left the building to the town, bless his heart, so the town had to decide what to do with the place. So far, two other mayors had passed, letting the building continue to decay.

The local historical society had been rallying to get the building designated as a National Historic Landmark. However, they had no ideas for it either, except to put the marker out front. Megan had a plan, but she needed the town behind her. Originally, she'd been talking to a developer, who wanted to turn the mill into condominiums, but that idea had soured when Meg realized the condos would probably be super expensive and provide few jobs and little income for the town. She'd been searching for an alternative when Gerry Ross, a hotelier from Indianapolis, expressed interest in buying the building, restoring it, and turning it into a hotel. It was the perfect solution, and Gerry and his team of five stood on the riser behind her, ready to share their vision.

She tapped the wireless mic that had been brought from the town hall to get everyone's attention, and after much milling around and chatter, folks finally settled down to listen. The hotelier had done this very thing with old buildings quite successfully in Indy, Cincinnati, and Lexington. He'd set out his plan on big boards that rested on easels along the sidewalk leading up to the building, and he'd brought a 3-D model that took up an entire conference table. Megan was impressed.

Hotel rooms were at a premium in River's Edge, a town

that depended on tourism to survive. Chautauqua, the big festival that happened in October, brought in visitors from all over the country, even from Canada, as did the Regatta, the boat race that was held on the mighty Ohio River every July fourth weekend. The rest of the year, tourists flocked to River's Edge for the wineries, the shops, the state park, and the atmosphere of the little river town—more hotel rooms would be a boon in her opinion. Now she and Gerry Ross just had to convince the town.

Low murmuring from the townsfolk began as soon as Ross ended his presentation, so Megan took the mic. "Folks, I'm going to tell you the truth. We need to do something with this old building. It's been sitting on the riverfront for years, just decaying. Mr. Ross here can restore it and turn it into something that will bring jobs to River's Edge, plus provide a place to house the tourists who come in for Chautauqua and the Regatta, the state park, and the Wine Trail. I've heard visitors complain when the state park inn was full or the other two hotels here in town were at capacity and they had to find a place to stay outside of town. That means they were eating breakfast outside town and shopping outside town as well."

Dot Higgins raised her hand. "What about the historic aspect of the place? We've been working on trying to get it marked as a historic landmark. I don't think we can do that if he turns it into a hotel."

Megan gave her a smile, determined not to get frustrated

with the same old arguments against selling the building. "Well, Dot, marking it as historic is a great idea, but if it falls into any further disrepair, we're going to have to tear it down. Does the historical society have the money to restore it and if you did, what would you do with it? How would you maintain it?"

"Well... um..." Dot's face fell.

"That's not the issue," Janet Knowles, owner of the Yarn Basket, declared. "We don't want some big company coming in and changing the ambiance of our town. The small-town charm is what we're known for all over the Midwest. If we start putting up fancy hotels and condos, that's not gonna work."

Rose Gaynor, who owned the Serendipity B and B, raised her hand. "How's this going to affect the rest of us who own B and Bs and hotels? And what kind of rates is he charging? Are we going to lose business?"

Megan turned to Janet first. "If you take a look at Mr. Ross's ideas, you'll see that he's keeping the original structure as intact as possible." Then she answered Rose's questions with a question of her own, keeping her tone as even as she could. "How many people did you turn away at Chautauqua, Rose?"

Rose bit her lower lip. "I don't know. Probably close to thirty or forty, but—"

Megan held up her hand. "Okay, and how many do you think the others turned away?"

Rose blew a breath into her bangs. "I imagine pretty close to the same. I get your point, Meg, but—"

"Hold on a sec, Rose." Megan looked over at Gerry Ross. "How many rooms in the new hotel again, Gerry?" She handed him the mic.

"We're planning on thirty-six rooms total, twelve on each of the top three floors. Downstairs will be a restaurant, a bar, a gift shop, and the front desk and lobby. We're going for intimate here," Gerry explained. "But as I said, we're still looking at about fifty new jobs, including day and night managers, housekeeping staff, restaurant staff, folks to man the front desk and gift shop—you get the picture. Peak season, we may require even more help. In addition to competitive salaries for the managerial positions, I'll be offering fifteen dollars an hour, health insurance, and other benefits to the hourly workers, including the folks in the restaurant. At Ross Group, everybody's family. We have a reputation for being a great place to work, and we'd like to continue the tradition here in River's Edge."

Megan couldn't help grinning at the startled looks on the faces of her townspeople as the words *fifty new jobs* and *health insurance* wafted through the crowd.

"You gonna use town people in these jobs?" someone in the back hollered.

Gerry nodded. "Absolutely. I need people working in the hotel who know this town and love it. You all will be my best marketing plan."

Dot raised her hand again. "But can we still mark it as historic even if it's turned into a hotel?"

Gerry Ross placed the mic back in Megan's hand. "Ma'am, come up and take a look at the elevations and the model we have back here. I think you'll be impressed at how much of the flavor of the building we can keep. I'm hoping we *can* get it marked as historic, even if we change its purpose. That's been done other places quite successfully. Why don't we explore that possibility together?"

More chatter ensued as the people absorbed the idea of turning the landmark into a profit-making venture. Some were still expressing doubts. Megan understood it was hard for the old-timers to imagine the cotton mill that had been a part of River's Edge for over a century as a hotel. Many of them had worked there before it closed down in the eighties, as had their parents and grandparents before them. Change was hard, she couldn't deny that, but her frustration level was growing.

"Hey!" A deep voice rose above the cacophony. When Megan looked up, her heart stuttered. Sean Flaherty stood at the back of the group, one hand in the air. "Listen people, Meg's not just talking about handing the building over to a developer and then we're out of it. She's talking about improving an area of our waterfront that looks like hell right now. And she's talking about bringing jobs in. According to Mr. Ross, they'll be decent-paying jobs with benefits." He limped slowly toward the dais. "We need this and it sounds like Mr. Ross and his team are ready to help us."

"But Sean…" Clyde Schwimmer, who owned Antiques and Uniques, scowled. "How do we know this place will fit in with the flavor of the town? I've got a good business here. We don't want some glass-and-steel structure tossed up along the River Walk. Plus, what kind of tax breaks are we giving him to do this?"

Sean grinned. "I've got a business here, too, Clyde, and frankly, I'd be damn grateful if the tourists who are doing the Wine Trail had a place to stay when other events fill up the rest of the hotels and B and Bs in town. I'm also hoping we can convince him to serve our wine in the new restaurant." He gave the group a dose of Flaherty dimples.

Megan blinked, too startled to speak for a moment.

What the hell is he doing?

Although she appreciated his support, she didn't need him to do anything more to encourage the older business owners who already still thought of her as *little Megan Mackenzie.*

She tossed Sean a raised brow, and took back her meeting. "Clyde, come up and take a look at Gerry's drawings and the 3-D model. They're amazing. The outside of the mill will look exactly the same as it does now, only better. The tax plan is in the material you got when you arrived. It's standard, nothing outrageous. We're not giving anything away here that we wouldn't give to any other new enterprise coming into town, I assure you." She waved a hand to direct the group to the line of easels and the round table that held the model. "Take a moment to chat with Gerry and his team and look at these plans. We can save this building, but it's never going to be a cotton mill again. Let's turn it into something we can be proud of, something that will enhance the riverfront."

As people slowly made their way up to examine the presentation, Megan sat on the edge of the dais and took a long pull on her glass of lemonade, waiting for the people to disperse enough for Sean to get to her. He wasn't using his walking stick and the limp, although noticeable, was subsiding. The late-afternoon sunlight glinted off his dark hair and stubble shadowed his jaw. He moved slowly, but he was handsome, tall, and straight as an arrow, and dammit, he took her breath away.

"You did a good job." He smiled, then leaned against the dais, stretching his right leg out in front of him. The brace showed below the hem of his shorts, but his calf was tanned and covered in a smattering of dark hair.

For some reason, Megan couldn't take her eyes off his muscled legs. How had she never noticed before how sexy his legs were?

She blinked and met his eyes, then nodded brusquely. "We vote next week. I hope everyone will be onboard. He's got somebody at the statehouse who will help him fast-track the permits, so things could be started pretty quick, I think."

"That means if they get the outside work done right

away, they can work on the inside over the winter and possibly have it done by next summer?"

His deep voice sent such a shiver up her spine, he might as well have been whispering sensual words of ardor instead of simply discussing the decrepit mill. He was his old self again though—no hunger in his eyes, no sign that anything out of the ordinary had happened between them.

So… fine. Okay, then.

She closed her eyes for a second, willing the tingle away because she was still ticked that he'd stepped on her toes in the meeting—unconsciously perhaps, but she needed to say something.

"You okay?"

When she opened her eyes, Sean was peering down at her face, his breath warm on her already-too-warm cheek.

She leaned away. "Yeah, just hot. It's August in Indiana. Things should cool off again soon." *The weather? Seriously?* How much more inane could she be? *Woman up, Meg!*

After a deep breath, she said, "Dude, listen, I appreciate what you were trying to do earlier, but please don't ride in on your white horse and try to rescue me when I'm running a town meeting. I had it, everything was fine."

His jaw dropped and he backed up slightly. "Meg, I-I didn't mean to—"

She held up one hand. "I know you didn't mean anything by it, but when you interrupt that way, it only reminds guys like Clyde and Noah that I'm not a part of the good-old-boys' network that's still around in this town. I've worked hard to get them to respect me as mayor, especially since I'm pretty sure none of them voted for me." She kept her tone neutral, but firm.

"Oh good Lord, it didn't even occur to me that you… that they…" He stumbled over his words before finally just offering a sincere, "I'm so sorry Megan."

"It's okay. Really." She glanced behind them at the townspeople milling around the model. "Looks like they're getting into it." Biting her lip, she debated for a moment, then charged ahead. "Sean, we need to talk about the other night."

SEAN WAS PISSED at himself for upsetting her in the meeting. That wasn't his intention at all. He'd pulled the oldest male stunt in the world, as if working with an office full of female attorneys had taught him nothing at all. Sam would've kicked his ass if she'd been here and he'd have deserved it.

Meg was clearly distraught—sweaty from the heat of the afternoon, and so tousled and adorable he could hardly resist taking her into his arms and kissing her stupid. However, this was neither the time nor the place.

Instead, still embarrassed for having upset her, he nodded curtly. "We do. Later. I have to get back to the tasting room. Chris is alone and once folks leave here, our place and

Mac's will be packed."

"But…" Her hands were so tightly clenched in her lap that her knuckles had whitened. "Sean, I—" Her lower lip trembled slightly.

He needed more time and a more intimate place than the yard of the cotton mill with half the town in attendance. At a loss for the right words to reassure her, he patted her shoulder, still fighting the urge to grab her and make love to her right there on the makeshift stage. "Are we okay here, Megs?"

When she gazed up into his face, the mix of distress and longing in her expression nearly undid him. "Of course we are, but—"

"Megan!" A distressed cry from the River Walk interrupted her. Sam was sprinting, as well as she could in a narrow skirt and heels, across the street toward them.

Meg jumped down from the stage, making a perfect balanced landing, and headed to her friend. "Sam. What's wrong? Is it Ali? Conor?"

"It's Dykeman's!" Sam was breathing hard. "I tried to call you"—she stopped to catch her breath—"but your phone went right to voice mail. I forgot you had this thing today."

"Dykeman's Orchard?" Sean handed Sam the glass of lemonade he'd nabbed from the table as he'd limped after Megan.

"Yes, their event barn burned down this morning." Tears

shimmered in Sam's dark eyes, while the breeze tugged at the auburn bun on her head. Accepting the cup from him, she sipped, then released a huge choking sob.

"*That's* what the sirens were. Oh, crap!" Megan led Sam back across to a bench on the River Walk and they settled on it, while Sean stood beside them, trying to figure out why this news, terrible as it was for Dykeman's, sent panic through Sam and Megan. Then it hit him.

Oh, Lord, the wedding!

Sam and Conor were getting married at Dykeman's in a month. "How bad is it? Are Leigh and Paul and Justin okay?"

Sam swallowed hard. "I just talked to Leigh. They're all fine, thank heaven, but they're canceling all their events for the rest of the year, so now I have a month to find a new venue and a new caterer and..." Her eyes grew round. "God, Leigh was even making our cake! What am I going to do?"

Sean watched as Meg slipped into emergency-friend mode. He couldn't help smiling. She was his old sensible girl again in less than five seconds. She patted Sam's shoulder. "Okay, deep breath, honey. We'll figure this out." She rose and paced for a moment.

Sean snapped his fingers. "Why don't we just do it at the winery?" He thought it was a stellar idea. Conor's first wedding at the winery had been a beautiful late fall affair.

Sam shook her head and tears rolled down her cheeks. "No. Conor and I chose Dykeman's deliberately so we wouldn't be repeating his and Emmy's wedding. We want this to be *our* day."

Meg gave him an exasperated look. "Didn't you and Conor discuss this when he asked you to be his best man?"

Sean shook his head. "No. He asked, I said sure and was glad when he said we weren't wearing tuxes."

Megan sighed. "Well, let's think, okay?" She paced some more. "It's too late to book the state park."

"I already thought of that." Sam sniffled.

Sean racked his brain. "What about the city park?"

"There's no shelter there, only the gazebo, so if it rains, we're screwed." Megan looked grim.

He suddenly had an idea. "How many guests, Sam?"

"Um, only family for the ceremony, then probably fifty or so for the reception. I didn't invite anyone from the firm; we just kept it to family and the people we're closest to here. We wanted it to be small." She gave him a curious glance. "Why?"

"What if we used the tasting room in town? It's plenty big enough for that size crowd if we use the inside, the screened porch, and the decks. You two could have the ceremony on the lower deck overlooking the river. And there are the awnings if it rains, and we can rent party tents if it pours." He hoped the tasting room wasn't too much like the winery to work.

Meg chortled, bouncing up and down on the balls of her feet. "Sean, that's brilliant!"

"But what about food and a cake?" Sam wasn't totally buying in, but Sean could see she was considering it.

Meg dismissed her worries with a wave of her hands. "You were only doing munchies and cake anyway. Paula can bake the cake and my dad can cater the hors d'oeuvres. Aidan and Brendan and Chris can pour wine and we'll set up some nonalcoholic drinks on the tasting bar."

"What am I going to tell my mother?" Sam leaned her elbows on her knees and covered her face. "She was already frustrated because we aren't getting married in her church in Chicago and having the reception at North Shore Country Club. Now, she'll be all *I told you so* and make my wedding day a living hell."

"No, she won't." Sean had seen that determined look on Meg's face as recently as last Friday night when she'd ripped Vin a new one. She held out her hand. "Give me your phone."

Sean couldn't imagine what Meg was up to, but it was sure to be interesting.

Silently, Sam handed her the phone.

Megan scrolled through the contacts before shooting a bewildered glance at Sam. "Where's your mom's number?"

"It's under Carlynne W. Hayes."

Sean couldn't help it. He chuckled as Megan's look of frustration was aimed at Sam this time.

"You have your mom listed under her full name?" Megan scrolled, stopping at the correct name and tapping it.

"You're calling my mom? Megan!" Sam tried to grab her phone, but Meg held it out of her reach.

"It's a month before your wedding and disaster has struck. You need your bestie *and* your mom. Trust me on this one."

Sam slumped back on the bench. "You'd do better to call my aunt Bette, but she and Joe are in Greece until the day before the wedding."

"Nope, your mom is a great organizer—you keep telling me that, so she can get her butt down here and help us organize this mess." Megan tapped the phone screen, then pointed a finger at Sean. "You're in this, too, mister; so emergency meeting tonight at the tasting room after you close. Be there. Bring the groom."

Sean caught a familiar gleam in Meg's brandy-colored eyes—she had a plan. He didn't want to miss this conversation, but when the bells at St. Agnes's church tolled four P.M., he had to get back. "She's going to take care of everything, Sam, I promise."

"She doesn't know my mother," Sam replied glumly.

He smiled as Megan began to sweet-talk Sam's mom. "She'll have your mother eating out of her hand in less than a day"—certain his heart was in his eyes as he looked at Megan, he blinked and turned back to Sam—"just like she does everyone she meets."

"Sean…" Sam eyed him with suspicion.

He held up one hand. "Gotta jet. See you later."

Ever so gently, he bumped Meg's arm with his as he walked past her and gave her a wink. The look in her eyes delighted him—alarm, confusion, hunger, tenderness… yeah, they *did* have to talk, but it could wait. They had time. He was coming home. They had plenty of time.

Chapter Fourteen

A BRISK KNOCK startled Megan out of the food coma she'd been in all evening. It had started with a bowl of her dad's German potato salad and a ham and cheese on rye and ended with two slices of key lime pie, which were heaven on a plate. She'd also opened her last bottle of Four Irish Brothers gewürztraminer and a bag of cheese puffs. Mamie was calmly licking away the last of the pie crumbs when the quick *tap, tap, tap* on her screen door made Megan nearly drop her Kindle; not a big deal since she'd only been staring at it blankly anyway. Sitting up with a groan from her comfy spot on the sofa, she peered at the time on her e-reader.

Eleven thirty. Who the hell shows up at the door at nearly midnight on a Sunday night?

Her first thought was her dad. Maybe something was wrong, although he'd appeared strong and healthy when she'd left him closing up the diner earlier. Or had something happened to Mère in Paris? If so, why didn't Dad just text or phone? Oh, God, unless it was really bad…

She steeled herself as the tap came again, more urgent this time. Giving her bike shorts and crumpled tank top a quick glance, she padded barefoot to the door. Her jaw literally dropped when she saw Sean Flaherty standing on the other side, swatting at the moths that were flying around his head.

"Open up. These moths are going to eat me alive." He rattled the latch on the wooden screen door.

Wordlessly, she unlatched the door and he slipped in. "I think one tried to fly into my mouth." He brushed at his lips.

"It's almost midnight." Megan glanced out into the darkness, noting that her dad's kitchen light was still on. *Great.* He'd see Char's Tahoe in the driveway and immediately know... oh, who cared? She was thirty-seven years old. She didn't owe her father any explanations. She shut the door and turned to Sean. "What are you doing here at this hour? Are you okay?"

"I wanted to talk to you." Sean's limp was more evident than usual as he walked into the small apartment. That meant he was tired or stressed. "I'm going back to Chicago tomorrow. I have a meeting with the firm on Tuesday. They want to make me an equity partner."

Meg gave him a questioning gaze. She had no idea what that meant. Wasn't he already a partner at Stark, Randolph, Smith, and Flaherty? "That's great news! But I thought you already *were* a partner. Your name is part of the firm name."

"They're going to invite me to *buy into* the practice," he explained, obviously catching her bewildered expression. "Right now, I don't own any of the practice, so I'm a partner in name only."

"Okay." She was still confused. "Well, good for you. Congratulations. I'm very proud of you."

Sean sighed, holding his hands up in an attitude of frustration. "Can we sit?"

She glared at him as she scooped up the knitted blanket and throw pillows on the sofa and with a jerk of her chin, indicated for him to take a seat.

He sat heavily, his bad leg out in front of him alongside the coffee table. In that moment, she hated him for smelling so delicious and for being so damn sexy. It wasn't right. At midnight, he should be tousled and needing a shower, like she was.

Then she noticed the detritus of her food fest—the pie plate, licked clean by Mamie, who had curled up in her usual spot on the seat of the wing chair. The Styrofoam container with remnants of potato salad clinging to the sides and a few crusts of bread, the crumpled cheese puffs bag, and the half-empty bottle of Conor's gewürztraminer lay atop a smattering of magazines and yesterday's River's Edge *Evening World*.

Oh, crap, he's going to know I'm still comfort eating after all these years.

She paused in her scurry to clean up the mess, then dropped everything back on the table.

What the hell, I've been able to eat him under the table for years. Besides, he's leaving tomorrow, so screw it.

She plopped down on the other end of the sofa and reached for her glass of wine—the only civilized note on the table.

Sean eyed her as she drained the glass. "Why yes, Megan, I'd love a glass of wine. Thank you."

Megan eyed him right back. "You know where the glasses are."

She felt a twinge of guilt as Sean sniffed, shoved up off the couch and, limping, retrieved a wineglass to pour himself a large measure of his brother's white wine. Crossing her arms over her breasts, she gazed at him. "Why are you here?"

He sipped, then sipped again. "Why are *you* so freaking hostile?"

"Hmmm, let's see." Megan held up one finger and then more as she listed what was wrong. "You rescue me from a terrible date, thank you by the way, and we practically do it on your stepmother's screened porch. Then you virtually ignore me for several days, however, you do show up to play Lancelot at my town meeting."

Sean's chin lifted and his brow furrowed. "I apologized for that already."

"I know and I appreciated it, but you also agreed that we needed to talk, and we haven't. We've spent every night together for the last week while we figured out how to save your brother's wedding, but you've just been treating me like your good buddy and then going back to the winery with Conor while I've been trying to figure out what the hell's going on here." She hated the sound of desperation in her voice. Taking a shaky breath, she just went for it. "Sean, we kissed."

His blue eyes sparked and his dimples showed. "I know."

"We don't kiss. That's not who we are." She flushed with heat, hating the red blush she was sure was spreading from her neck to her face. "We're friends, Sean. We should be able to get past this... this thing that's going on between us."

Sean simply stared at her. "Is that what you want? To get past it?"

She swallowed hard and closed her eyes for a moment, holding her face to the cooling breeze from the ceiling fan.

When she looked at him again he was still gazing at her, his blue eyes piercing. At last, he crooked his finger in a come-hither motion. "Come here."

Megan forced herself to sit still, even though those smoldering eyes were drawing her in. "No, dammit."

"Come on." Sean's voice caressed her. "Let me kiss you."

She raised her chin defiantly. "Why do you want to kiss me?"

His grin nearly turned her inside out. "Because you're adorable and sexy and I've been dying to kiss you every moment I've been with you since you left Char's that night. Hell, sweetheart, I almost attacked you on the dais at the town meeting. But what could I do? We haven't been alone for more than two minutes and we need to work this out before we bring the rest of the world into it. Besides, I know you're going to taste like key lime pie and, man, I love key lime pie."

"Sean, what's going on?" Megan moaned, dropping back against the corner of the sofa. "What the hell are you doing?"

Sean dropped his hand in his lap. "Lately? Harvesting early grapes with Conor. Bottling port. Working the tasting room in town. Helping handle wedding plans. Going to PT," he enumerated, ticking each item off on his fingers, before giving her a crooked smile that sent a shiver up her spine. "But mostly, fantasizing about you and trying to figure out what I'm going to do with my life."

"Yeah?" She couldn't help herself; she pulled up and scooched a few inches closer. It was the fantasizing remark that got to her because she'd been doing the same thing. "What *are* you going to do with your rest life, Sean?"

In one swoop, he reached for her and pulled her into his arms. "Oh, trust me, I've got a plan, but I need to go back to Chicago to make it work. That's why I'm here, to talk to you before I leave. Right now though, I'm still dying to kiss you." He put one hand on her face and gently tugged the elastic from her ponytail with the other. "Can we just... for a minute..." Tunneling his fingers under her hair, he tipped her face up and kissed slowly from her forehead, down her nose, and skipping her mouth, dropped another soft kiss on her chin. His tongue followed her cheek, then the line of her jaw, and his breath warmed her ear.

At last, his lips found hers and a touch that began as tenderly as a whisper immediately turned into a soul-shattering kiss. His mouth took hers with desperation, and God help her, her desire matched his. Their tongues met in a frantic duel as his hands slipped down her back to her hip, reaching for the hem of her tank top.

She thrust her fingers into the too-long hair at the nape of his neck—tilting her head, so he could take her lips again and then again. All clear thought was gone and what was left was raw hunger. She wanted his hands on her, his lips on her...

WHEN SEAN'S FINGERS touched the bare skin at Meg's waist, he drew back slightly to look into eyes that had darkened to the color of rich maple syrup. God, he wanted her, wanted every curve, all the soft lushness that was his Megs.

His Meg.

That was how he'd come to think of her these past few weeks. He was so proud of who she'd become while he'd been away. Who'd have guessed back in high school that she'd be *mayor* of River's Edge one day?

He traced the line of her spine and the flare of her hip and knew without a doubt that *this* was exactly what he'd come for, no matter what he'd told himself on the drive over. It was supposed to be a check-in—just letting her know he was driving to Chicago tomorrow and he'd be back before the wedding. He'd decided before he knocked there would be no touching and certainly no kissing. Just talking because, man, they needed to figure this out, and because he had the feeling she wasn't at all sure she was prepared to take their friendship in a new direction, even though every look she'd given him since that night on Char's porch told him she wanted him just as desperately as he wanted her.

But then she opened the door, his best bud, all bristly with anger, regal, curvy, and long-legged, her peachy skin showing beneath the snug bike shorts and tank top she wore, and abruptly, the game, as Sherlock would say, was afoot. He couldn't think about anything except kissing her, getting his hands on that warm flesh, and damn the consequences. They could figure it out later, after the heat subsided. "God, you're beautiful." His breath hitched at the sight of her eyes soft with lust and her lips red and swollen from his kisses.

He licked her lips, tasting wine and, sure enough, key lime pie, and she opened her mouth to his as she wrapped her arms around his neck. A groan rumbled in his chest and he let his hands wander under her tank top, around her ribs, cupping firm round flesh as he pushed her back on the sofa.

Suddenly, searing pain knifed through his right thigh, and he yelped.

Megan shoved him away. "Oh, God, my knitting!" Leaping up, she reached between them and yanked out a pile of bright yarn that had two metal knitting needles sticking out of it. "Sean, I'm so sorry! Are you okay? Did it hurt you? Are you bleeding?"

He stretched his leg out, one hand covering the spot,

where under his shorts, the pain was so intense it brought tears to his eyes. Lying against the back of the sofa, he gritted his teeth, swallowing the bellow that had lodged in his throat.

Megan knelt beside him, her fingers gently pushing back the hem of his shorts, pressing on the area, scanning his leg for any signs of injury. Her other hand rested on his left thigh, so high up, he couldn't help the natural reaction that was happening, in spite of the pain in his right leg.

"Megs, I'm fine." He grasped her hand that was unconsciously rubbing his thigh and hauled her up off her knees, although, heaven knew he would have loved for her to stay right there and fix the unholy ache that had developed at the sight of her blond head so close to his lap.

As she rose and straightened her shirt, he reached for his wine and took a deep drink, willing his body to find some semblance of normal. Even though the pain in his thigh was subsiding, the other ache was still going strong and watching the soft skin of her stomach disappear as she jerked down her tank top didn't help it any.

"I'm so sorry. I forgot it was there." She scooted Mamie out of the wing chair and dropped into it. "Sean, look—"

He put his hand up to stop her because he could see in her face what she was about to say. "Don't." He didn't want to hear her say that she was having doubts about *them*.

Hell, hadn't he been tossing his life around like a pair of dice for the last four months? Go back to Chicago? Stay in

River's Edge? Be a partner in a law firm? Be a partner in a winery? Life in the city? Life on the river? But the one thing—the only thing—he knew for certain was he wanted Megan Mackenzie. In his arms, in his bed, in his life. He was positive they were right together—that one conviction drove all the other choices. Conor was right, love was a good reason to turn his life upside down. He was pretty sure he was about to do exactly that and he wanted Meg onboard.

She shook her head, her expression suddenly unreadable—sympathy? Longing? Sadness? It worried him that he couldn't tell because, before, he could always, *always* read her.

"Sean, I have no idea what's happening between us. Whatever it is, I don't trust it."

He leaned forward, the wineglass dangling from his fingers. "Why not?"

"Because I don't know where it's coming from."

"That's easy, Meggy. It's coming from here"—he touched his chest, keeping his voice even with effort—"I want you. I think I've always wanted you. I just didn't know it."

She gazed at him for a long moment. "I think you're scared. You've just been through a hellish trauma and you came home to heal, where life is quiet and predictable and safe."

"So? Your point?" He wasn't certain where this was headed, but he was pretty sure it wasn't going to end with him in her bed tonight. That was okay, except that it could also mean there was a chance he'd never get there, and the very thought sent a pang of anguish through him.

"I'm part of the safe. That's all." She gave him a half-smile. "Good old dependable Meg. Your buddy who's always there for you. Now suddenly, she's driving you out of your mind with lust? I don't think so, pal."

He bit his lower lip. "Friendship can turn into more, Megan. It happens all the time."

"After all these years?" Megan's voice was laced with doubt.

"Do you want me?" Sean wasn't sure that challenge was a good idea but he didn't know where else to go.

"No." She said it so quietly and so fast, he knew she was lying, and he knew she knew she was lying.

"Liar."

She sighed. "Don't you get it? I don't want you to want me because I'm *safe*. I want you to want me because I drive you insane. Because you're madly in love with me."

He lifted his hands from his lap—the ache had lessened, although it was still evident. "For God's sake, look at me!" He hoped the wry smile would warm her up.

Megan simply shook her head. "That's biology."

He pushed up from the sofa; he couldn't sit still another second. "No, it's chemistry. *Our* chemistry, Megan."

With a sigh she rose and grabbed the knitted blanket off the rocking chair where she'd tossed it earlier. Wrapping it around her shoulders, she folded her arms over her breasts—a sure sign she had closed up. "I've been down this road too many times before. I can't go down it with you... not with my best friend. I couldn't bear losing you." She marched to the door, opened it, and stood there, shoulders taut, spine stiff, but he could see tears shimmering in her eyes. "Go back to Chicago, Sean. Go back to your real life. When you come home for the wedding, maybe things will be normal again."

Sean took two steps to the door, then stopped to stare at her. She was serious. She was sending him away. He tried once more. "Megan, I love you."

She offered him a small sad smile. "I know. I love you, too. I always have. You're my best friend."

His chest hurt. The ache had moved to his heart. He resisted the urge to grab her, make her see what was burning inside him. That wouldn't be a smart move—not with Megan. "I'm going up there to turn in my resignation. I'm coming right back and I'm staying. I'm going to work the vineyard with Conor, help Sam at Harry's firm, and you and I are going to be together. You'll see, I—" He stopped.

She didn't believe him. He could tell from her expression that she was seeing the old Sean Flaherty, the kid who had been so full of plans and dreams for two best friends on those long hot summer days when they'd trimmed grape vines together or sat by the river, talking endlessly about their futures. The dreamer who'd planned their hike across Europe after high school graduation, the trip to Ireland and

Scotland to trace their roots in between freshman and sophomore year in college, the cruise to Alaska before their senior year... All the things that had never happened because when they went away to college, he spent his summers interning in the city, while she came home to River's Edge to help in the diner.

Tears shimmered in her eyes. "No, Sean. You belong in Chicago. You'll see that when you get back there."

"I belong here...with you."

She simply shook her head.

As he left, he paused and cupped her cheek, brushing away a tear with his thumb. "You may not trust this," he whispered, "but *I* do. And very soon, you will, too, Meggy. I promise you that."

Chapter Fifteen

"WE'VE ARRIVED!"

Megan spun around on her stool at the sound of Sam's announcement. A warm late-August breeze blew in as her friend opened the diner door, accompanied by one of the most beautiful older women Meg had ever laid eyes on. Even more elegant than Mère and that was saying something.

She had to be Sam's mom because first of all, except for the age thing, she was the very image of Samantha Hayes—in miniature. Where Sam was tall, shapely, and long-legged, this woman was petite and perfectly formed. Her sage-green linen slacks and silk sleeveless top matched exactly and her canvas espadrilles were the same soft green tone. Rich auburn hair threaded with silver was pulled into a neat chignon on the back her head, her makeup was flawless, and she had deep brown eyes just like Sam's. However, the woman's expression did not match Sam's usual sunny demeanor at all—her lips were pressed tightly together and her entire body seemed as taut as Duane Wilson's guitar strings.

Meg rose and greeted Sam with their usual hug. "Hey,

sister!" After a quick squeeze, she extended her hand to the woman, who stood, grimly clutching a designer handbag. "Hi, I'm Megan Mackenzie, Sam's maid of honor."

"Hello. Carlynne Hayes." Sam's mom's handshake was firm and quick as she eyed Megan up and down.

Megan quelled her instinct to shrink back from her fierce gaze and instead, grasped Carlynne's shoulders lightly and gave her a kiss on each cheek, French style. "Welcome to River's Edge. Dad's closed the diner early this evening so you two are free to spend some uninterrupted tasting time."

Lips still in a forbidding line, Carlynne tolerated the embrace, then stepped away to scrutinize the retro décor of Mac's Riverside Diner. "*This* is where we're tasting wedding hors d'oeuvres, Samantha?"

Behind her mother's back, Sam made a face that nearly undid Megan. "Yes, Mother. I told you, Meg's dad, Mac, is an incredible French chef and—"

"A French chef cooks *here*?" Carlynne's voice dripped disdain and disbelief.

"A French chef *owns* this joint." Mac, who had eschewed his usual jeans and T-shirt for pressed khakis and a button-down shirt, covered by a red RIVERSIDE DINER apron, for once simply opened the gate that led behind the counter, and strode to the three women. "Hey, Sam. Got everything ready for you back in the kitchen." His stormy-gray eyes swept over Carlynne.

Megan knew that look. This lady was going down. Dad

didn't take kindly to people looking down on his diner or his food. She hoped he wouldn't be too snarky.

Once again, he surprised her. Extending his hand, he gave Carlynne the smile that had melted hearts all along the river. "I'm Graham Mackenzie, but everyone calls me Mac. You must be Sam's mother. Delighted to have you here."

When Carlynne placed her hand in his, he turned it over and pressed a quick kiss on her knuckles. "Come into my kitchen…" And he led her away, glancing over his shoulder at Megan and Sam, who stood by the door, dumbfounded.

"Said the spider to the fly," Megan murmured for Sam's ears only.

Sam gave her a side-eye. "This should be interesting."

Megan watched as her father took Carlynne back to the kitchen, where he'd spent the better part of the early-morning hours preparing several delectable canapés for the bride and her mother to sample. She jerked her head toward the kitchen. "Come on, I can't wait to see how this turns out."

"He's in for a battle. She's a tough one." Sam kept her voice low as they sauntered toward the kitchen. "She made the chef who catered my high-school graduation party cry. It smells heavenly in here, though."

"Oh, Dad can hold his own." Megan hoped she was right because as far as she could see from where she was standing, Carlynne had yet to crack a smile.

Mac pulled an apron off a hook by the kitchen door and

without any fanfare at all, tied it around an unsuspecting Carlynne's tiny waist before tossing two more in Megan and Sam's direction. "Here, girls, put these on. My kitchen is spotless, but we don't want to take any chances with those pretty summer tops."

Aproned, Sam and Megan peered in at a gorgeous display on the prep table in the center of the kitchen. Even Carlynne's eyes got bigger as she walked around the table staring at the trays of appetizers.

Mac grabbed four small plates and napkins. "Everything's finger food per your request, Sam. Start here"—he pointed to a cut-glass salver full of what appeared to be salmon dip on toast—"with the smoked salmon rillettes. They're made with the Coho salmon I catch every April in Lake Michigan. I smoke them on my patio at home and they're ready for all kinds of great dishes. I add crème fraîche and shallots to this old French recipe and serve it on rye toast."

Megan and Sam watched as Carlynne nibbled a corner of one canapé delicately, her perfectly arched brows furrowing. Then, to Meg's amazement, she popped the whole thing in her mouth, chewed, swallowed, and closed her eyes. A long moment later, she opened them again. "My goodness, Mr. Mackenzie. This is delicious. *You* made this?"

"I made everything on this table." He stopped her from taking another salmon delicacy from the plate. "No, no, first taste each one and then we'll eat leftovers for a late supper. I have a table set for us out in the diner with a couple of bottles of Conor's wine we can open. We can discuss which ones you want for the wedding while we eat."

Megan glanced out at the dining room. Sure enough, he'd set a table for two with linen, his Waterford crystal wine stems, and the Bernardaud French porcelain plates he'd brought from Paris years ago. Very fancy.

Only two places? Interesting.

Megan grinned, grateful she'd warned her dad what to expect with Sam's mother. Carlynne Hayes had no idea, but she didn't stand a chance once Graham Ian Mackenzie turned on the charm.

Together, Mac and Carlynne went around the table as he described each hors d'oeuvre in detail while Carlynne tasted and hung onto his every word. Megan and Sam simply followed along behind, also tasting and groaning at such amazing treats as warm spiced olives, lobster toast with avocado, figs with bacon and chili, herbed squash comfit, and shrimp and rosemary crostini. Dad had outdone himself and was looking pretty smug as Carlynne's cold stony demeanor thawed a little more with each new dish. Mac had even included his famous baguettes with truffle butter, and tiny seared beef tenderloin and grilled pork tenderloin mini sandwiches for the die-hard Hoosiers in the crowd.

As they ended at a goat cheese crostini with date-and-cranberry relish, Carlynne clasped her hands together over her breasts in apparent ecstasy. Breasts that Megan had already noticed were still pert, either because of a great bra, plastic surgery, or just damn good genes. Either way, Dad was clearly into her because he hadn't been able to take his eyes off Sam's mom since she'd walked into his kitchen.

"Mr. Mackenzie, you are a culinary wizard." Carlynne finally broke a real smile and her face lit up so beautifully that even Sam looked stunned. "I'd love for you to make every single one of these for the reception, however we must pick only a few, otherwise you'd spend the next three weeks in your kitchen just cooking for us."

Mac's eyes gleamed. "I can't think of a more worthy endeavor, Ms. Hayes."

Carlynne touched Mac's arm. "Oh, please, call me Carly, all my friends do."

Her dad grinned and Megan could see the pleasure in his face that he'd won this round. "Okay, Carly it is, but no more Mr. Mackenzie. I'm Mac."

Carly turned the full force of her incredible smile on him. "May I call you Graham? It's one of my favorite Scottish names."

"You may call me anything you like as long as you promise to stay and join me for a late supper."

"I'd be honored." Carly untied the apron and handed it to him as Megan and Sam simply gaped at the pair of them. "Where may I powder my nose?"

Sam shook her head in obvious disbelief. "Come on, Mother, I'll show you the restroom."

As they walked out of the kitchen, Megan turned to her dad, who leaned against the counter with a smug expression on his handsome face. When she was sure Sam and her mom were out of earshot, she whispered, "Oh my God, Dad. That was *unreal*." Then she stepped over to throw her arms around his neck. "You're brilliant!"

Mac returned the hug. "Oh, honey, I've been handling women like Carly Hayes for years. Food and of course, my scintillating personality. Gets 'em every time." He grinned and offered a little self-deprecating shrug.

Megan returned the grin. "Okay, now the trick is to *keep* her enthralled until after the wedding. Sam deserves a happy day."

Mac took up the nearly empty plate of salmon toast, grabbed tongs, and began piling other hors d'oeuvres onto the platter. Carrying the tray of goodies around to the wait station across from the main counter, he took off his apron, yanked the bandanna from his head, and ran his fingers through his thick gray hair. "You two girls get outta here. *I'll* take care of Mom." He carried the plate to the elegant table he'd set and with a smile and a wink began opening wine. "It'll be my pleasure."

"OH. MY. GOD." Sam kicked off her sandals and curled her feet underneath her on Megan's overstuffed sofa. "I can't believe your dad. He *is* a wizard, just like Mother said. He bewitched her." She shook a finger at Mamie, who was lounging on the back of the couch, eyeing the coffee table. "Don't even think about going for that plate of goodies, Mrs. Eisenhower."

Megan poured iced tea into two tall glasses and handed one to Sam. "Dad can be a charmer."

"Charmer? Meg, *I* was ready to stay and have dinner with him. If I wasn't madly in love with Conor, your dad could've totally had me tonight." Sam took a long gulp of tea, then reached for one of the nibbles that Megan had packed up for them before they left the diner. They'd gone out the back door, but passed by the window on the way to Megan's and caught a glimpse of Mac and Carly seated across from one another in the dimmed restaurant. "He's not going to break her heart, is he?"

Megan snorted. "Not hardly. She's only going to be here three weeks and Dad's good, but he's not known for his fast moves. Honestly, I can't remember the last time he even had a date."

"Well, he certainly has one tonight"—Sam chewed her lower lip—"with *my* mother! Holy cats, we could end up sisters!"

Megan cracked up. "Um, I think you're letting your imagination run a little wild, don't you? My dad's not going to sell off the Riverside and move to the North Shore of Chicago, and your mom sure as heck isn't leaving her high-rise apartment to move to River's Edge, no matter how charming *Graham* Mackenzie may be."

"Did you believe that? *Graham's one of my favorite Scottish names.*" Sam's imitation of her mother's breathy voice was spot-on. "Lord, Conor's going to howl at this story. He was so nervous meeting Mother, he almost hurled his breakfast this morning. If your dad has charmed her, can you imagine how she's going to react to Ali when she meets her?"

Megan reached for the last fig with bacon and chili. "That kid'll wrap her around her little finger just like she has all of us."

Sam just nodded and smiled the dreamy little smile that always appeared on her face when she thought of Conor and Ali. Megan couldn't help the twinge of envy that washed through her. She wanted to be able to smile that way about someone; lately though, that wasn't looking too possible. Vin was absolutely out of the picture and Sean, even if he'd meant what he said before he left, had been gone for days without so much as a phone call or a text.

A car door slammed. "Do you think they're back already?" Megan rose to peer out the screen door. A car she didn't recognize was in the driveway.

The driver hopped out with a yellow mailer in his hand and gazed around before he noticed the sign with the house number and an arrow pointing up to Megan's apartment above the garage. He zipped up the steps just as Meg turned on the porch light against the darkness that had fallen.

"Megan Mackenzie?" The young man wore a polo with the name of a courier company Megan didn't recognize.

"Yes." She glanced over her shoulder at Sam, whose brown eyes shone with curiosity.

"This is for you. Sign here." He held up the package and an electronic tablet for her to sign with her finger.

"Thank you." Megan re-hooked the wooden screen door, watching as the man hopped back down the stairs, typing on his tablet after he slid back behind the wheel.

Sam leaned forward on the sofa. "What is it? Who's it from?"

"No clue." Megan turned the package over in her hands, feeling the shape of a square box inside. "There's no return address."

"Well, open it."

"What if it's a bomb or anthrax or something?" Megan held the package away from her. "It didn't come from UPS or FedEx. It's just *this* with my name and address written on it. I'm a city official. What if somebody's unhappy with me?"

Sam rolled her eyes. "For pity's sake, you're the mayor of River's Edge, Indiana, and everyone here adores you. You think Dot or Clyde is gonna send you a letter bomb? Who delivered it?" She rose and took the package from Megan, peering at the writing on the outside of the package. "That writing looks familiar."

"Some courier company called 4-Star, according to the guy's shirt."

"I'd swear that's Conor's printing. He never writes cursive. It's not quite right, though. His doesn't lean back like that." She shook the package. It thunked a little, but it didn't rattle. Whatever was in there had a little weight to it.

"Why would Conor *send* me something?" Megan took the mailer back. "He could just bring it to me." She examined the blocky black letters. The printing did look familiar. "Call him. See if he sent me something via courier."

Megan held the package gingerly in her hands as Sam made the call, spending more time than she thought was necessary checking in with Conor, although that was typical because there was always a moment or two of mushy stuff before they could hang up.

Sam grinned as she put her phone in her skirt pocket. "Open it."

"Is it from Conor?"

"No, but he says to open it."

"He knows what it is?"

Sam chuckled. "Just open it. It's okay."

Frowning, Megan pulled the tab at the top of the package. Inside was a square white jeweler's box tied up with a yellow ribbon. She tossed the mailer aside, untied the ribbon, and lifted the lid. Inside was a folded note.

Remember the day I taught you to skip stones on the river and you lost your friendship bracelet on the shore? You cried because you thought it was gone forever. I went back that night with a flashlight and found it.

The next day, you were drooling over Duane and his new guitar, so I put both our bracelets away, thinking one day, maybe we'd wear them again... Sean

She handed the note to Sam, then took out a purple, red, and yellow woven-string friendship bracelet that she hadn't had on her wrist since she was thirteen years old. Under it lay a round flat stone, exactly like the ones Sean had found for her to skip across the water that day. Before she could even think, her phone chimed with a text message.

When she checked it, there was a picture of Sean's strong wrist encircled with *his* woven-string bracelet—the one she'd made for him in camp that long-ago summer. The one that matched hers. The message underneath said, *Maybe it was fate we left the tie ends extra-long. Always ever...*

She caught her breath, taking the bracelet out gingerly and running it between her thumb and index finger. Her heart stuttered as she remembered the day they'd woven them—both of them hot and sweaty in the crafts area of the fellowship hall at church camp. Sean's camp girlfriend had just broken up with him, and Meg had cajoled him out of his cabin to come do crafts with her. Grumpy and recalcitrant, he'd agreed, however not before he'd made her promise to buy him a bag of Skittles at the snack bar and not the regular Skittles either, the tropical ones because he loved the green kiwi flavor. Oh, and he wasn't making any stupid hats.

He'd cheered up as they worked together and even

shared the Skittles with her. Later, they'd tied the friendship bracelets onto each other's wrists in a solemn ceremony by the lake that included a vow to always have one another's back, no matter what. Sean had wanted to cut both their wrists with his scout knife and rub their blood together, but Megan had been afraid she'd faint, so they'd settled on a spit handshake. Hands clasped, they'd recited a silly couplet Sean had made up on the spot.

Always ever, failing never, Sean and Meg, best friends forever.

Megan didn't realize she'd said the words aloud until Sam's "Awww, that's so sweet," brought her back to the present.

Heat rose to her cheeks and she blinked back the tears stinging her eyelids as she tucked the bracelet back into the box and replaced the lid. "Sean Flaherty's the biggest packrat I know. Honestly, I'd hate to see his closets. The guy is incapable of throwing anything away." Surprised her voice sounded normal even though her heart was racing, she tossed the box on the table by the door, started to turn away, then picked it back up again. Opening it, she pulled out the bracelet and held it against her wrist.

Damn Sean, anyway. What was he trying to do to her?

Chapter Sixteen

HANDS FOLDED UNDER his head, Sean lay in bed, watching the moon drift over the Chicago skyline outside his apartment window. It was past midnight. Megan had gotten the package four hours ago according to the text from the courier. He grabbed his phone from the nightstand beside him and checked the screen again. Nothing. No response to his text. No call. Nothing. His chest felt heavy. He was a stupid, sentimental fool.

Shoving the covers off, he carefully swung his legs over and sat on the edge of the mattress. His thigh ached. Not enough for pain meds—he'd flushed those weeks ago, but maybe a beer would help him sleep. He had to get some rest. The movers would be here in a few days, and although they would pack up most all his belongings, he still had his personal boxes to pack. Careful to avoid the empty cartons covering nearly every square inch of floor space in his bedroom, he padded to the kitchen. Without flipping on the light, he opened the fridge, nabbed a frosty bottle of Founders, twisted off the cap, and settled on the couch in the dark.

It had been a long day and it was proving to be an even

longer night. He'd spent his last day in the law offices of Stark, Randolph, Smith, and Flaherty, a name that would be changing soon. He chewed his lower lip as he considered who'd be the next number four on the banner once his name came down. No doubt one of the eager beavers who'd wished him well with a hearty fake smile today. Only good old Charlie Smith was truly going to miss him. The man damn near had tears in his eyes when Sean had turned in his resignation two weeks earlier, and the long-time partner had talked hard and fast, trying to convince him to stay.

Charlie—hell the whole office—was sure it was the shooting that was driving their most accomplished attorney away and maybe that was a small part of it. But as Sean had stood in the conference room, eating cake and drinking champagne with the partners, associates, and staff at his farewell party, he'd had the epiphany he'd subconsciously been waiting for since long before that fateful day on the steps of the courthouse.

Chicago wasn't home anymore. Actually, it had *never* been home, and as much as he'd enjoyed being an attorney, this firm wasn't where his heart was, either. He'd miss his colleagues, sure, however, they weren't *his* people. Even after twelve years of working with them every day, he really didn't know them all that well. He'd never had the easy familiarity at the law firm that he shared with Harry or Mac or Clyde Schwimmer or Noah at Barker's Hardware. He'd never believed his fellow lawyers had had his back the way his brothers did or Char.

Or Meg.

The overwhelming sense of peace that traipsing the vineyard with Conor brought or the sense of rightness he had strolling the River Walk with Megan had never been present in his life in Chicago. As he looked around at the all the suits and all the sharp, attractive women he'd worked with for so many years, he wanted nothing more than to escape. So as the champagne flowed and the voices and laughter got louder, he'd slipped out, stopping by his office to grab his briefcase and rucksack before making one more stop in the lobby. The barbershop.

Ron had greeted him with the usual, "Hey, Mr. Flaherty," as he brushed off the shoulders of a man Sean vaguely recognized from the brokerage on the seventh floor. "Sure have missed seeing you around here. How's the leg?"

Sean waited for the other patron to leave before he spoke. "Leg's doing well, Ron. I just wanted to stop by and say thanks for everything."

Ron looked askance. "Okay. You're welcome. For what?"

Sean laid an envelope on the counter by one of two chairs in the small shop. "For twelve years of great haircuts."

"You going somewhere?"

"I'm going home to Indiana."

Ron quirked one thick gray brow. "Permanent?"

"That's the plan." Sean nodded and smiled. "You see, there's this girl…"

NAN REINHARDT

"There's always a girl." Ron chuckled.

"This one's pretty special."

"Good for you, Sean." It had been the first time Ron had ever called him by his first name. "You need a trim before you go back to meet this special lady? Getting a little shaggy back there."

Sean grinned and gave the barber a firm handshake. "I think I'm good, thanks. All part of my new noncorporate look. So long, Ron."

And *that* had been the saddest farewell of the day.

On the sofa next to him, his cell phone lit up and chimed. He almost spilled his beer as he grabbed for it. His breath caught in his throat.

It was Meg. *"I can still skip a stone with more bounces than you, pal."*

He grinned. *"I don't think so,"* he thumbed back, setting his beer bottle on the table next to the couch.

"Remember how the circles widened into each other when the stones skipped across the water?" she texted.

His heart sped up as he imagined her, all tousled and warm, in the big brass bed he'd helped move into the apartment above her dad's garage all those years ago. Did she still have her great-grandmother's old quilt? The one with the all the colors? A spasm of longing shot through him at the mental picture he'd created and every nerve and muscle tightened.

"I do," he typed. *"That was your favorite part."*

Almost a minute went by before his phone chimed. *"Still*

190

is."

He took a deep breath before thumbing, *"Can I call you?"*

Another endless moment later came, *"Thanks for the memory, Sean. Good night."*

That was a *no. Dammit.*

He hadn't really believed she'd fall into his arms over an old bracelet, a rock, and a fond childhood memory. Even so, he couldn't help feeling disappointed. He wondered if she'd even put the bracelet on. He touched the braided threads on his own wrist. It wasn't coming off any time soon since he'd gotten it on with a great deal of difficulty—ended up using his teeth to knot the tie ends together.

He looked at his phone screen one more time.

Thanks for the memory...

He smiled as he thought of the box he'd dug out of the closet at Char's and brought with him when he drove up to pack. He wasn't giving up. There were plenty more memories.

MEGAN LOOKED UP when the door to her office in city hall slammed shut. Sam stood there, her back pressed against it, eyes wide, and panting like she'd run all the way from Harry's Victorian house on Adams Street. Meg's breath hitched. What on earth had happened now? It was less than a week until the wedding and last night, as they'd all sat around the diner after closing, they'd gone over every detail.

The affair seemed to be on track.

Sam's mother, Carly, had turned out to be a godsend with a checklist, rounding up decorations, ordering the cake, confirming reservations for several round rental tables and chairs, as well as plates, flatware, and beverage glasses for the nonalcoholic drinks that would be served. Flowers were ordered, everyone's clothes were all arranged, and Chris and some of the other men in town were ready to hang decorations Friday night. Heck, the woman had even charmed Justin Dykeman into volunteering his horse and carriage to pick up the bride and her entourage, such as it was, and take them the few blocks from Sam's apartment above Harry's offices to the Four Irish Brothers Winery tasting room on the river. Everything was set.

She rose from her chair, her heart thumping. "What's wrong? What's happened?"

Sam dropped into the armchair across the desk from Megan. "My mother didn't come home last night."

Megan blinked, her thoughts still muddled going from the cotton mill contract she'd been focused on to Sam in such a hurry. "What? Is she okay?"

Sam blew out a frustrated breath. "Oh, she's just dandy. Came in as I was getting ready for work. I was two minutes from calling Duane and asking him to put out an APB on her when she just strolled in reeking of bacon, carrying two coffees, and wearing jeans and a diner T-shirt."

Megan was still confused. "Okay, good. So she's fine."

Sam leaned forward in her chair, her auburn hair falling over her cheek. "Meg, she *spent the night* with your father! Then she got up with him at four thirty in the morning and helped him open the diner." Sam jumped up and paced to the window and back, peering out at the town square. "Right this minute, she's grabbing a shower, then she's taking our laundry out to Conor's because *eww, laundromat*. So, okay, in some ways, she's still Carlynne. But this afternoon, she's taking Ali to Posey Pushers, so she can be measured for her flower tiara. Mother wants Ali to pick out her own flowers for Caroline to put on her headband, then they're going to Target to get the kid a new pair of dressy shoes. Target! My mother has never seen the inside of a Target." All this said in one breath left Sam wheezing.

"Target's amazing. She'll be in heaven."

"Not the point." Sam coughed, then glared at her.

Megan dropped back in her chair and rubbed her face. "Look, this all sounds great. What's the problem?"

"The problem is, who is this woman and what has she done with my mother?" Sam stalked back to her chair. "*My* mother doesn't do laundry. She doesn't eat bacon or drink coffee. She doesn't deal with children on any level, *ever*. And yet, last night, she told Ali to call her Mimi. *Mimi* for God's sake! And worst of all, she *spent the night* with your dad! As far as I know, until now, she's only had sex once in her life and I was the result. Now, Carlynne Waters Hayes, who never steps out of her Carolina Herrera suits and her Christian Louboutin red-soled pumps, wandered in this morning in a pair of old jeans I can only assume she found at the new consignment shop that just opened up over on Mulberry, sandals, and a Riverside Diner T-shirt looking... well... *satisfied*."

Megan chuckled. "The magic of River's Edge."

"The magic of Graham Mackenzie, you mean." Sam shook her head. "She's smiling, Meg! I mean full-on, teeth-showing smiles. She *hugged* me this morning and not a little social hug either, a real mother-daughter hug."

"That's great! Maybe she's turned over a new leaf. She's only fifty-something. Never too late to change your life."

"I don't trust it." Sam scowled. "Something's going to happen and she's going to turn back into zipped-up, too-cool Carlynne and it'll probably happen Saturday, two hours before Conor and I step in front of the minister."

"Oh, chill out. She's finally enjoying life." Megan dismissed Sam's fears with a wave of her hand.

However, it was disconcerting to hear that Carly and her dad were... *Argh!* Megan couldn't make herself even think about *that*. Not because she couldn't imagine her dad having sex; she could, although she'd rather not, but because she didn't want him to get hurt and this situation had pain written all over it. Carly was heading back to Chicago in another week and Dad was going to be brokenhearted. She suddenly got an insane mental picture of her and her father, leaning on the bar at the Beer and Badger, crying into their

Jameson together.

"Nice daisies." Sam stopped fuming long enough to touch the huge bouquet of white daisies that had graced Meg's desk for the last couple of days. "Who sent them?"

Meg raised one brow. "There is always a chance I bought them for myself, you know? We don't have to wait for someone to buy us flowers. We can get our own flowers."

Sam put up both hands. "Um, sorry, Oprah, didn't mean to offend your feminist sensibilities. I assumed—"

"Sean sent them, okay?" Unable to meet Sam's curious gaze, she grabbed a pen and began doodling on the notepad on her desk.

"Okay." Sam eyed her. "And these?" She pointed to a pile of small origami cranes before picking up a couple and tossing them gently in her hand.

Megan lifted her eyes. "Also from Sean. They came with this." Sheepishly, she held up a Pez dispenser with the head of Snoopy on it.

"I love Pez!"

"Help yourself."

Sam reached for the dispenser, released a candy disk, and popped it in her mouth. "Strawberry!"

"We used to give each other Pez for Christmas every year. He loved *Spiderman* and I loved *Peanuts*. He mastered the art of shooting the stupid candy out of the plastic thingy into his mouth. I could never do it." Megan smiled at the memory.

Another damn memory.

Sam's eyes narrowed as she crossed her legs and settled back into the chair. "What's going on? Conor talks to Sean almost every night, but it's almost always vineyard stuff, I think."

Megan chewed her lower lip, not sure at all whether she was ready to talk about Sean and her, not even with Sam. If she talked about it, would that make it real? "He-he's wooing me, I think."

"*Wooing* you? That's an interesting term to use."

"I can't describe it any other way and I'm not even sure that's what it is. I've gotten all this stuff from him since he left—memory stuff, things to remind me of who we once were. That bracelet, a can of silly string, a huge bag of Skittles." She sighed. "The daisies—my favorite flower—I'm sure to remind me of that time in high school when I was pissed at him about some stupid thing and he stole daisies from Harry and Dee's front yard and brought them to me. Harry threw his slipper at him. God, we laughed our butts off.

"The origami cranes. He used to make them in algebra class, out of notebook paper, when he should've been paying attention. Then he'd bribe me with them to help him do his homework because, seriously, math was totally beyond him. I can't believe he still knows how to make these silly things." She picked a paper crane up off the desk and cupped it in her palm. "Last night I got a mixtape. Can you believe that? I've got to scare up my old boom box to listen to it, but if I know Sean, it's a bunch of the music we all used to dance to on his parents' screened porch. I taught him how to slow dance so he could ask Francie Schwimmer to the junior prom."

Sam pursed her lips. "What do you think he's trying to accomplish?"

"I think he's trying to prove to me that I'm in love with him," Megan whispered, "that I always have been."

"How's he doing?"

Megan dropped her head into her hands as tears burned behind her eyelids. If she admitted this to Sam, did that mean she'd have to 'fess up to Sean when he got home for the wedding? And if she did, then what? He was in Chicago. She was here. "Oh, hell, Sam, I knew that before he sent the first memory. I knew when I heard he'd been shot." Tears choked her words. "I-I couldn't e-even breathe."

She sniffled and swallowed the lump forming in her throat before she continued. "I've been denying it since he got home, chalking those feelings up to sympathy, sisterly affection—you name it. Heck, I even thought I was past it because of how much I wanted Vin, but maybe that was just me subconsciously believing I could bring Sean and me back to our old easy friendship." Tears spilled over as she raised her head and met Sam's compassionate gaze. "But jeez, Sam, I want him. I can't stop thinking about him."

"Oh, honey." Sam rose and came around the desk to wrap her arms around Meg. "This is a wonderful thing, isn't it? Because Conor says Sean is nuts about you."

Megan leaned her head on Sam's shoulder. "What if he isn't really? Remember the conversation we had about me being *safe*? Like River's Edge? Like the winery? Like his brothers? What if that's all it is and this thing fizzles out? Then I've not only lost the love of my life, I've lost my oldest and dearest friend."

Sam hugged her and gave her a little shake before resting her behind on the edge of Megan's big antique desk. "There are no guarantees in life or love, Megs—you know that. Sometimes, you just have to take a leap and trust that the other person is going to be there to catch you, or at least swim alongside you when you land in the water. I did it and look…" She extended her arms as her smile lit up the office. "Conor did it; he even brought his daughter along for the swim. Hell, look at my mother! Talk about taking a giant leap!"

She folded her arms over her chest, clearly debating her next words. "Sean's been unfulfilled in Chicago for a long time. I saw it when I worked with him. He was restless, frustrated, always seeking. The only time he was truly happy was when he was anticipating coming home for a while. When he'd get back to the firm, he'd be Mr. Grumpypants again. I've never seen him as peaceful as he is here. With *you.*"

"Oh, God, Sam. I don't know. I just don't know." Megan shoved her chair back, stood, and wandered to the window. The square was quiet, the morning bustle over, but it would hum again when the bells at St. Agnes chimed the noon hour. Then her citizens would meander to lunch—maybe soup at Mac's or a croissant at Bread and Butter or a brown-bag lunch from home in the park or perhaps just a walk along the river since it had cooled down in the past couple of days.

Her citizens. This was her life. These people. This town. It had always been that way. But the hole inside her had been there, too—an empty place that hadn't been filled in a long time. Not since Sean Flaherty had left River's Edge to pursue his own dreams.

She sensed Sam's presence behind her before her friend grasped her shoulders. "Take a leap, Meg. You and Sean belong together. He knows it, I know it, hell, even Ali sees it. And you know it, too, if you just open up your heart."

Chapter Seventeen

FOR THE FIRST time since she'd moved out, Megan actually tapped on her dad's back door and waited for him to show up, peering in the window as he padded into the kitchen in just a pair of khaki shorts. As he flipped on the overhead light, she considered him for a moment. The man was good-looking, no question about that—a neat gray-and-white streaked beard, overlong graying brown hair, and a firm, muscled chest. When he smiled at her curiously as he opened the door, she couldn't help noticing what a great smile he had. No wonder Carly had fallen so hard so fast.

"Why you knocking, kiddo? It's always unlocked." Mac held the screen door open for her as she slipped past him into the kitchen and inhaled the delicious aroma of whatever he was cooking. Bread for sure and something with basil and shallots and… was that chicken?

"I didn't know if you had company." Heat burned her cheeks. *Embarrassed? In front of Dad, of all people.* "I didn't want to interrupt," she mumbled.

He chuckled. "Carly's at Sam's dealing with dresses. She'll be by later." Tugging open the fridge, he took out a couple of beers and held one up. "Care to join me?"

Megan shook her head. "I don't think so, thanks."

"What's up?" Mac grabbed the bottle opener from a drawer and popped the cap on his beer.

"I'm looking for my old boom box. Do you still have it?"

He took a long drink of beer, then swiped the back of his hand across his lips. "It should still be in your room. It's pretty much the way you left it."

Megan laughed. "Lord, Dad, you really ought to turn it into an exercise room or something. It's been years." With a quick wink, she scooted up the stairs.

On the way to her old room, she glanced into her dad's bedroom, noticing the pile of rumpled sheets on the floor next to his freshly made bed. Once again, heat crept up her neck to her cheeks. Her dad washed his sheets once a week—every Sunday morning before he opened the diner. Like clockwork. This was Wednesday night. She scurried past the open door.

Not going to think about that.

In her bedroom, she located the ancient cassette player on her desk. As she rummaged in the drawers trying to find the power cord, she stopped to gaze at the corkboard above her head, still filled with photographs and concert tickets, play programs, 4-H ribbons, and other detritus from her school days. Amazing how many of the photos were of Sean or her and Sean.

She caught her breath as one photo in particular captured her attention. She wasn't sure who'd taken it, probably Joanie Thomas or Duane Wilson—those were the two people she and Sean hung out with the most among their group of friends. Mostly likely Joanie; she'd been a camera fiend. She'd eventually turned it into a career and now did photo shoots for an advertising agency in New York. She plucked the tack from the corner the photo, turned on the work light, and held the picture beneath it.

It was the two of them—she and Sean—treading the low stone wall in front of the Warner mansion, the restored home-turned-museum that overlooked the Ohio River and the beginning of the River Walk. He was standing behind her, his hands on her hips, keeping them both balanced as they gazed, laughing, into one another's eyes. Her head was tipped to the side and back so she could see him, and her long blond hair hung over his arm. His dark hair was shaggy and his expression showed his whole attention was focused on her. They were young, maybe sixteen. The tenderness in his blue eyes sent an arc of longing straight through her, and her own adoring expression took her breath away.

Her reaction was so visceral, her knees went weak and she dropped into the old desk chair, starting at the loud *skreek* the legs made when it scooted across the hardwood floor. She remembered that day; recalled feeling small and protected in the circle of Sean's arms. Remembered being rendered completely powerless by his grin; and then the sensation of being adrift, untethered, when they'd jumped down and he'd dropped her hand.

Adrift.

That was how she felt right now, how she had been feeling for longer than she could remember. Not aimless or unhappy—her job, her dad, her friends, this town, even Mamie kept her life fulfilled and satisfying most of the time. But she hadn't felt truly *whole* in ages, as if a piece of her was missing somehow until… She stared down at the photo. Until Sean Flaherty had come home, hurt and needing her. The empty space had filled up, and when he kissed her, it had overflowed.

She almost jumped out of her skin when her dad cleared his throat. He was standing in the doorway, the pile of sheets and some towels from his bathroom in his arms and a small knowing smile on his lips. They stared at one another for a few seconds before she muttered, "I can't find the power cord."

"I've got batteries downstairs if you need them."

"Thanks." She stood up, tucking the picture into the back pocket of her shorts. "I'll take them."

"Why do you need that old thing?" Mac stepped aside and allowed her to pass in front of him as they headed down the stairs. "I thought you had music on your phone."

"I-I've got a cassette I want to listen to."

"Good Lord, honey, why don't you just download the music?" He followed her into the kitchen, tossing the pile of sheets and towels into the adjoining laundry room before reaching into a drawer by the back door to pull out a package of D-size batteries. "*D*s, right? How many? Seems like I remember that thing took several."

Megan opened the back of the machine. "Eight. Do you have that many?"

Mac glanced at the drawer. "Yup. Here you go." He held the packages just out of her reach, a question in his eyes.

She sighed. "Sean sent me a mixtape."

"Interesting." Mac took the boom box from her arms, slid the back cover off again, and loaded the batteries into the compartments—a job that would have taken Meg at least a full five minutes as she figured out which direction to put them, even though she knew the negative end always went on the spring. "Seems like something's been delivered here at least once a day for the last couple of weeks. What's going on, honey?"

Megan accepted the player from him and planted a quick kiss on his bristly cheek. "Dunno yet, Dad. But when I figure it out, I promise I'll tell you."

He placed one big hand on her shoulder. "Sometimes, the best stuff in life happens when you least expect it, Meggers." He chucked her chin affectionately before pulling her into his arms, boom box and all, for a warm hug.

Her throat closed as the fragrances of Irish Spring soap and baking bread and basil filled her senses—all the scents that were her dad—and she rested her head on his shoulder for a moment. Then she stepped out of his embrace. "I love you, Papa. Enjoy your dinner with Carly. It smells heavenly."

He jerked his head toward the industrial-sized stove. "*Poulet aux herbes de Provence.* You're welcome to join us."

"Thanks; I already ate." She gave him a thumbs-up and scurried out the door to avoid any more questions she wasn't prepared to answer.

MEGAN HIT PLAY on the tape machine for the third time, flipped her pillows over to the cool side and settled back to listen again. Turned out, it wasn't a mixtape at all, only Survivor's "The Search Is Over," recorded three times on each side. It had been an oldie when they danced to it as teenagers, however, the sweet melody was an easy one to teach Sean to slow dance to and they'd played the song over and over that autumn as he got comfortable with the simple steps. Truth was, back then, she'd been so focused on helping him learn to rumba she hadn't paid attention to the beautiful lyrics about a man who finally realizes he's actually in love with his best friend.

The song sent hunger for him skittering along every nerve in her body, and she longed to hear the sound of his voice, feel his lips touching her ear. She hopped out of bed, got the jeweler's box from the dresser, and took out the string bracelet. Fingering the woven threads, she laid it over her wrist. The ties were still plenty long enough; maybe she could remember how to do the sliding knot she'd mastered at camp all those years ago. After several false starts, she finally managed a perfect sliding knot in the cord. With a satisfied smile, she slid it over her hand, and tightened the bracelet on her wrist. It looked right at home against her tanned skin. Suddenly, as if by some magical psychic connection, her phone chimed with a text from Sean.

"Are you awake?"

She responded instantly. *"Yes."*

Nothing more for a couple of minutes as she stared at the screen, willing him to text her back. Then her cell vibrated in her hand.

SHE ANSWERED IMMEDIATELY, her voice breathy and soft like she'd been anxious for his call. *A good sign.* Sean glanced around his barren bedroom as he settled back on his pillows on his last night in Chicago. His boxes were all packed and the movers would be there in the morning. He'd cut short a farewell night on the town with Vin and the other guys from the poker game, anticipating instead a long conversation with Megan, if she answered her phone. She had, thank heaven, and suddenly, he was tongue-tied and shy and feeling a little like a teenager calling his crush for the first time.

"Hey." He really ought to come up with something a bit

MEANT TO BE

more creative and interesting. "Are you in bed?"

"Yes. Are you?"

He smiled. That was exactly where he hoped she'd be and why he'd waited until almost midnight to call her. Meg had always been a night owl, especially if she was reading a great book or had gotten enraptured by some romantic comedy on TV. "I am. What are you wearing?"

She chuckled. "Is this an obscene phone call?"

Every muscle tightened and heat flooded his insides. "Well, that depends on you. Would you like it to be?"

"Um... maybe. When did you turn into such a perv, Sean Flaherty?" Her voice was low and sexy.

"Not a perv, sweetheart, just a guy who can't stop thinking about the last time he saw you." He kicked off the sheet. "You had on those hot bike shorts and a tank top and if I'm not mistaken, you were braless. Your hair was tumbling down over your shoulders, you smelled like key lime pie, oh, and you had orange cheese-puff powder on your cheek—"

She gasped. "Oh, no, did I really?"

He laughed. "It was the sexiest thing I'd ever seen."

"Why didn't you say something?" she scolded. "You could have at least offered me a napkin."

He squirmed, his boxers suddenly feeling too snug, and he was grateful he'd left off the brace before he got into bed. "I knew I was going to kiss it away, which I did, if you recall."

She was quiet for a moment. "You did," she whispered

finally, and even more softly she said, "I miss you."

"I'm coming home tomorrow. I can be on your doorstep by the time you get done mayoring for the day."

"Tomorrow night's Conor's stag and Sam's bachelorette," she reminded him. "And I have a meeting with Gerry Ross and the historical society to sign the contracts for the hotel at five thirty, so I won't be done *mayoring* until it's time to go meet Sam." Disappointment laced her tone.

"Crap," he muttered. "Well, the *stag* will most likely consist of the four Flaherty brothers, Mac and Harry drinking Da's chambourcin and eating sausage, bread, and cheese in Conor's living room since I'd pretty much forgotten about that part of the best man duties." He took a deep breath. "I haven't been able to focus on anything except getting back to you."

"Oh, Sean…" Her sigh was sleepy-sweet.

"Meg, I want to touch you. I need to kiss you." He was probably setting himself up for an uncomfortable night but he couldn't help it. He wanted her so much, he could barely breathe imagining her next to him in his bed. "It's driving me crazy thinking about you."

She was so quiet he worried she'd ended the call.

"Meg? Are you still there?"

"Yes. I-I—" She stopped and so did his heart.

Please God, don't let her say she doesn't want this. That she doesn't want me.

"I'm longing for you too, Sean." The words were almost

inaudible, but he was certain he'd heard her correctly.

"Longing? Really?"

"Yes. I can't stop thinking about you kissing me." Her voice strengthened. "I'm so mixed up. I want you so much and it feels so wrong, but it feels so right, too. What are we going to do?"

Sean's heart nearly burst and, mentally, he cursed the three hundred miles between them. The ache that had started at the sound of her voice grew almost unbearable, so he stood up, shucked out of his boxers, and dropped back onto the bed. "Oh, Meggy, me darlin', how I wish we were together right now, instead of having to wait until tomorrow. I could show you all the things I'm dying to do to you."

There was a pause, a rustling of sheets, and then her voice, warm and deliciously sensual. "Why don't you tell me about them now?"

Chapter Eighteen

"GOD, I'M SO sorry we're late!" Sam breezed into Mario's Pizza, with Ali in tow and Char, her mom, and her aunt Bette on her heels. The bride plopped down in a decorated chair at the head of the table next to Megan, exhaled a huge breath, and grinned at the women gathered there. "Hi, everybody!"

They'd shoved several tables together to make one long banquet table that would accommodate all the women Meg had invited to Sam's last night of being single. Everyone had managed to show up—Tierney, who came in uniform because she was on break from the fire station, Paula, Sandy from Posy Pushers, Dot and Mary Higgins from the quilt shop, Janet from the Yarn Basket, Rose Gaynor from the Serendipity B and B, and Norma and Sheila, the waitresses from the diner. Also in attendance were Harley Cole, Ali's preschool teacher, Alice, Sam and Harry's office manager, and the paralegal Gia Bishop, who'd given Megan a surprised and grateful look when she'd extended the invitation on the sidewalk outside the diner a couple of weeks earlier.

Megan held no animosity toward Gia, although Gia had

been quick to tell her that she hadn't heard from Vin since that awful weekend. It didn't matter. Vin was nothing more than a bad memory, one that had been replaced with the delicious here-and-now, thanks to Sean.

Carly stood at the end of the table and held up a shopping bag. "I have gifts for everyone! First, for my lovely daughter." She reached in the bag, drew out a white T-shirt, and unfolded it. *Bride* was emblazoned across the front in hot pink letters.

Shaking her head, Sam took it and pulled it on over her tank-style sundress. "Thanks, Mom. I love it!"

Megan couldn't believe her ears. She'd never heard Sam call Carly anything other than *Mother*, and that was usually said with a grim smile or an eye roll. Now, Sam's smile for Carly was real and full of affection as mother and daughter exchanged a warm hug. Megan couldn't help getting a little misty.

The magic of River's Edge.

Carly emptied the rest of the contents of the bag onto the red-and-white checked tablecloth. The woman howled with laughter—Carly had a T-shirt for every woman present, all appropriately labeled. *Maid of Honor* for Megan, *Aunt of the Bride* for Bette, *Mother of the Groom* for Char, and *Flower Girl* for little Ali. There were even *I Baked the Cake* and *I Did the Flowers* shirts for Paula and Sandy respectively, with *Friend of the Bride* shirts for everyone else, all in hot pink script on lightweight pink knit T-shirts.

Carly's own shirt proudly proclaimed her honored position as *Mother of the Bride*. The woman didn't flinch a bit when tugging her shirt over her head pulled a couple of pins out of her elegant chignon. She simply swept the loosened curls back up into the knot, thrust the hairpins in, and turned to help Char get into her T-shirt. Sam gave Megan a sideways glance and a grin.

As everyone else donned their shirts, Sam leaned toward Megan so she could hear her over the chatter of the restaurant. "I thought we'd never get here. Good Lord, what a screw-up."

Megan, popping with curiosity, smoothed her shirt over her sundress. "What happened? Is everyone okay?" And by *everyone* of course she meant Sean, who'd texted her from a rest stop on I65 a couple of hours earlier to let her know he probably wasn't going to get to River's Edge in time to see her before all the pre-wedding festivities began.

Sam waved one newly manicured hand as she passed Ali off to Carly, who, with Char's assistance, got the child shirted and settled into a chair between the two grandmothers.

Megan could see those two were in their element together, fussing over the little girl, while Ali was eating up the attention.

"Oh, everyone's okay," Sam assured her, "it's just that the moving van came to the winery instead of going to the storage unit Sean rented up on the highway. When he pulled into Char's, they were arguing with her and trying to offload his furniture into the driveway."

Megan blinked. What on earth was Sam talking about? *Moving van? Sean's furniture?* Her incredulous "*What?*" came out an octave higher than her normal tone and loud enough that everyone at that end of the table stopped to gape at her.

Sam frowned. "What *what*? It's okay. He got it worked out. He and the guys are up there now, helping the movers load it all out into the storage unit."

The voices around her shifted to background noise as Megan's heartbeat thrummed in her ears. Unable to speak, she just stared numbly at Sam.

"Meg?" Sam whispered. "God, you're white as a sheet. What's the matter?"

Megan shoved her chair out, grabbed Sam by the elbow, and pulled her up. "Can you guys excuse us for just a sec? Quick wedding emergency." Pushing a protesting Sam in front of her all the way to the door, she stopped when they got to the sidewalk outside of Mario's.

Sam jerked her arm away. "Jeez, Megan, what the hell is wrong with you?"

Megan swallowed hard and tried to control her erratic breathing. "Sean's actually moving back?" she finally managed.

Sam's brow furrowed and she peered at Megan in the last light of dusk. "Well, yeah. That's why he went up to Chicago—to quit and get his apartment packed."

"He left his job?" Meg's voice squeaked again as she tried desperately to wrap her head around this new reality. *Sean has really moved back to River's Edge.* "But...but they offered him a full partnership—he was buying into the firm. Wasn't he?"

Sam shrugged. "They did. He turned it down and resigned instead. He's going to help Conor at the winery and take on some of my cases since I'm overwhelmed and Harry's sure to get elected judge in November." She reached for Megan's hand and pulled her closer, her expression incredulous. "He didn't mention any of this to you?"

Meg closed her eyes, trying to get her heartbeat to slow down as she recalled that last night before Sean left for Chicago. "He did... yes. He told me he was going to resign and move back here, but"—she raked her fingers though her hair—"he said it in a moment of... of emotionality, and I didn't believe him. I thought he was, you know, just reacting to everything that's happened to him. Plus, I was upset and so was he and we were both a mess. I never thought he'd actually do it. I was sure he'd get back to Chicago and realize how much he missed his life there." She shook her head, trying to get a clear thought going. "We've texted a little bit and we talked last night. He said he was coming home, but I thought he meant for the wedding, not for good."

"He didn't mention moving when you talked?"

Heat rose in Megan's face. "No. We...we talked about other stuff."

Sam gave her a curious glance. "What could possibly be more important than the fact that he was moving back home?"

Megan stared at her sandals, her cheeks burning. "Never mind. It-it doesn't matter." She gave her friend a little push. "Go back in. I'll be there in a sec."

Sam tipped her head to peer into Megan's face. "Oh. My. God! Did you two…? *On the phone?*" Then she gave her a shrewd little smile. "Was it fun?" Her brown eyes twinkled.

Knowing it was pointless to try to deny Sam's assumptions, Megan grinned back. "It was amazing. Go. I'm going to text Sean. I'll be right in."

Sam gave her a quick hug. "We're gonna be sisters one way or another, aren't we, Madam Mayor?"

Meg returned the hug, then gave her a light swat on the shoulder. "Not that I'm aware of. Just go."

Pulling her phone out of her pocket, she inhaled the scent of pepperoni pizza that wafted out when Sam opened the door. Her thumbs hovered over the screen as she debated what to say to him. She started to type, stopped, deleted the message, typed again, deleted again. Nothing sounded right. What exactly did she want to say to him? *We have to talk.* Yes, they did need to talk, but not in a text. This wasn't a texting kind of conversation. She gave it up and pocketed her phone.

Better to wait until they were alone and face-to-face, even if that meant waiting until after the wedding.

THE FLAHERTY BROTHERS were where they always ended up when they were together—in the wine cellar, perched on wooden barrels, drinking Da's chambourcin. Mac, Harry, Sam's uncle Joe, and the rest of the guys had left after a long night of loading Sean's furniture into the storage bin, then coming back to the winery for food, wine, and a few rounds of poker, which Mac and Sean had won handily.

Sean chuckled as he sipped the delicious red wine. Affection filled his heart as he gazed at his brothers. Nothing in Chicago beat hanging out with family. "Poor old Harry—he was really expecting strippers tonight."

Conor grinned. "Yeah, when he left, he told me *bachelor parties just ain't what they used to be*. I told him Sam and I had agreed no tackiness tonight, and he gave me the most pitying look. Almost like he was considering revoking my man card."

Brendan snickered. "Good ole Harry. God, I haven't been to a stag with strippers since I was in my twenties. Do guys even do that anymore?"

Aidan shrugged. "The last stag I went to was at the Beverly Wilshire—no strippers. Lots of tuxes and expensive champagne, though, and a bunch of guys standing up telling stories and mocking the groom. It reminded me of those old Dean Martin roasts we used to watch on late-night TV when we were kids. Remember those?"

Sean laughed. "Oh yeah, with Don Rickles and those other old-time comedians. Man, Da loved those roasts; he had videotapes of them, I think. I wonder what happened to those old tapes and his VCR. You think Char still has them somewhere? We should watch them again—the ones you see on the comedy channels now aren't nearly as much fun as those were."

Conor swept the room with one arm. "The last stag I went to was my own and pretty much, it was exactly like this one, except I think Da won at poker. But we all ended up right here, doing exactly this." He tipped his glass in a salute to his brothers. "To Da. I really wish he'd been able to know Sam."

The others nodded agreement and clinked glasses. "To Da! *Sláinte!*"

Brendan raised his glass again. "To Conny, who found love a second time. May you and Sam be blessed with eternal love and may you provide us with more nieces like the inimitable Miss Ali and even a nephew or two."

Conor chuckled as the brothers toasted and drank. "You guys need to get busy. I'm the only one of us who's ever been married and I'm starting on number two. You gotta catch up. Sam and I can't provide the entire next generation of Flahertys."

Sean didn't miss the pointed look Conor shot his way, but he merely smiled. Time enough to talk to his brothers about Megan. It was too new to hash over. And yet it was as familiar and right as anything he'd ever experienced.

He swirled the rich wine in his glass. "Con, I want to learn to do this—make wine like Da's and yours. I've been reading like crazy. All Da's books and online, and it's fascinating. Will you teach me?"

"Of course I'll teach you." He held up one finger and winked. "You gotta start at the bottom though—cellar rat—and work your way up."

"I'll hose off floors, pick grapes, prune, clean tanks and the crusher, whatever you need. I'm home now." He smiled around the circle of faces so dear to him. "I'm just happy to be here and be a part."

Aidan hopped off his barrel to reach behind Conor for the bottle of wine and refilled everyone's glass, running short as he got to Sean. "Crap. It's empty. Hang on." He trotted to the stack of cases across the room, pulled another bottle of chambourcin, and then nabbed Da's old wood and iron corkscrew from the wall in the office. Holding it up, he glanced at Sean and then gave Conor a long look, a sly expression on his face. "Okay, so if I can open this one, using Da's corkscrew and not eff up the cork, Conor has to agree to let me buy the new tanks and French oak barrels." He eyed Conor. "Deal?"

Sean held his breath and watched Conor's reaction. Never once had Aidan been able to use Da's antique corkscrew correctly. His incompetence was practically the stuff of family lore. Every single time he tried to use it, he broke the cork, and he was tipsy enough from the wine they'd already consumed that chances were very good, he'd screw it up again. But he and Aidan had rehearsed this, counting on the fact that their brother, the winemaker, could rarely resist a challenge, so he said his line. "Aidan, don't make that bet with him or we'll never get new equipment." He turned to Conor. "Conny, just accept the damn money, okay?"

Conor pursed his lips and his blue eyes, so like Sean's own, narrowed. "No. Let him give it a shot. If he can do it, I'm all-in. If he screws it up, we put off the new tanks and barrels until spring and you, my little cellar rat, will be installing a new racking valve on number three while I'm on my honeymoon."

Sean shook his head firmly in the negative. "While you're on your honeymoon, I'm going to be busy trying to find a place to live. I won't have time to repair that broken-down tank."

Conor just raised one dark brow. "Go on, Ace, open the wine." He smirked as he used the nickname they'd given Aidan as a kid. "Oh, and remember to remove the foil first."

Aidan looked down his nose at Conor. "I was raised in a winery, you douche, I know how to remove the foil."

Conor chuckled. "Yeah. However, can you remove it with Da's corkscrew?"

"That's not part of the deal," Sean objected, trying to sound convincing.

Conor just sipped, then crossed his arms over his chest.

"Those are my terms."

Brendan stood up, nearly stumbling as he teetered over to Aidan. "C'mere kid, I'll help you get the foil off." His words slurred as he tried to take the bottle but instead tripped on the floor drain and almost fell headfirst into Aidan.

Aidan turned away from him, shielding the bottle from Brendan's grasping fingers. "Smooth, Bren. Did they teach you that move in spy school?"

Bren recovered his balance, sighed, and went back to his barrel, heaving himself up. "How many times do I have to tell you I'm not a damn spy? I'm a political analyst."

Aidan brought the bottle and corkscrew over to his own barrel. "Of course you aren't." He gave Bren a meaningful wink. "Not a spy. *Riiiight.*"

Brendan spun around, practically tipping off the barrel he was perched on. "Guys, tell this goofball I'm not a spy."

Sean, basking in the warmth of these precious moments when all four of them were together, simply laughed. "Hell, dude, I dunno what you do out there in DC. Do you, Con?"

"Nope." Conor shook his head. "And I'll bet if he tells us, he'll have to kill us, so stop annoying him, Ace, and just open the damn bottle."

Brendan threw up his hands and shook his head in disgust as Aidan carefully, or as carefully as a guy who was halfway in the bag could manage, cut the covering off the top of the bottle with the tip of the corkscrew. He waved the shredded foil. "Ta da!"

Conor nodded, nibbled calmly on a cracker, and gestured with his wineglass. "Very nice. Now open the bottle."

Sean thought he looked remarkably relaxed for a guy who was about to lose a thirty-thousand-dollar bet, but on the other hand, he knew something that Conor did not. Aidan had been practicing in LA for over a month with an antique corkscrew just like Da's that he'd discovered on eBay, and he had pretty much mastered it. He and Sean had cooked up this little bit of theater when they'd talked a few days ago, hoping they'd get the opportunity to use it while they were all together for the wedding. Conor had yet to agree to accept any investment from Aidan, even though tank number three was still leaking.

Sean played the concerned big brother pretty well, and he caught Aidan's eye as his youngest brother made a huge production of centering the point of the corkscrew exactly perfect before he rotated it into the bottle. He kind of wished Aidan was a little less drunk, because they hadn't figured *that* into their plan. The kid was just going to have to sober up enough to do this right. Hell, he was an actor; he could pull this off. When Sean looked around, he noted that he wasn't the only Flaherty brother holding his breath. Bren watched with narrowed eyes and even Conor wasn't as cool as he pretended to be if his white knuckles were any indication.

Smooth as silk, Aidan cranked down the old corkscrew, tugged the cork, whole and unharmed from the bottle of chambourcin, and held it up. "And that, my brothers, is how it's done in LA." He swaggered over to Sean and poured some wine into his now-empty glass before stopping in front of Conor. "I'll do an electronic transfer Monday. Or, you can just let *us* order the tanks and barrels. Show us what we need and we'll take care of it while you and Sam are in Aruba."

Conor gaped at Aidan and then at Sean. "You guys planned this! Somehow he's been practicing. C'mon, confess."

Sean returned Conor's astonished expression with a smirk of his own. "Bro, I'm not replacing that valve when it's the whole damn tank that's leaking. It's a waste of effort."

Conor just shook his head. "You guys are killing me." He raised his hands in surrender and allowed Aidan to pour more wine into his glass. "Okay, you win. New tanks, new barrels. *And* new grapes. The Frontenac vines go in next spring, as soon as that field down there thaws enough to plant." He pointed a finger at Sean. "We'll work on the trellises whenever we have decent weather over the winter, and we'll go together to the Finger Lakes to buy the vines. I've already talked to a guy at a vineyard in Geneva who's promised me hardened plants in March."

Sean grinned even as he blinked back tears of joy. Healing had been a hard journey, but he'd found himself in the process, and now he knew exactly what he wanted—to work with Conor and Sam, to stay in River's Edge, and to make love with Megan Mackenzie every night for the rest of his life.

Home at last.

He raised his glass. "To the Four Irish Brothers Winery, the pride of Donal Flaherty. May we always give him reasons to be smiling down on us from heaven."

Laughing, he and his brothers brought their glasses together. "*Sláinte!*"

Chapter Nineteen

"UNCLE SEAN!" ALI squealed and twisted away from Megan, who was crouched next to her, once again straightening the little girl's tiara of daisies and baby's breath. "You *are* home!"

When Megan glanced up, Ali had thrown herself onto her uncle's legs and his eyes met Megan's as he scooped the child up into his arms with a *whoop*.

A shiver of excitement eddied through her and desire pooled in her belly at the look of hunger that darkened his blue eyes to almost navy. She rose and smoothed her dress over her hips, a move that brought a quick intake of breath from Sean.

Ali kissed him soundly on the cheek. "I didn't see you last night because we had a girls' slumber party at Sam's, but Sam said *you* were at a slumber party at *my* house." She giggled. "But for boys, not girls." She held up her little hand, fingers splayed. "Look what Mimi did! Pink! My favorite!" When he didn't respond immediately, she took his chin in her other hand and turned his face toward her—away from Megan. "Look!" she insisted.

Sean blinked and focused on Ali, while Megan's insides quivered at how obviously hard it had been for him to tear his eyes from her. They needed to talk because how were they ever going to keep this new element of their relationship a secret if their faces shouted their attraction to the world any time they were in the same vicinity? On the other hand, according to Sam, everybody already suspected it anyway, so maybe the whole secret thing was moot. Lord, clear thought was impossible when she was in the same room as Sean.

"Wow, that's beautiful, Ali." Sean's voice sounded a little husky as he regarded his niece's pale pink nails. "Now, I kinda wish I'd had Uncle Aidan do mine for today." His big hand enveloped Ali's tiny one. "What do you think? Red? Or maybe yellow and blue to match my tie?"

Ali chortled. "That's just silly, Uncle Sean. Boys don't wear nail polish."

Megan reached for her. "Sometimes boys do, kiddo. As a matter of fact, after the wedding remind me to tell you about a time Uncle Sean wore black nail polish to a Halloween party when we were in high school."

Ali made a face. "Black? Eww!" Then she touched the string bracelet on Megan's wrist. "Hey, your bracelet matches Uncle Sean's! Look! You're bracelet twins!"

"So we are." Megan avoided Sean's hot gaze as she set Ali on the floor, straightened the tiara and the bow on the back of her dress, then gave her a little pat on the butt. "Head out and find Mimi, honey. She's got your basket of flower petals.

We're going to start pretty soon."

"Okay." Ali opened the door to the small cottage on the riverside tasting room property that usually served as a storage shed, however today it was acting as a launch area for the event. The carriage had just arrived at the venue, and Megan had hopped out with Ali who desperately needed the bathroom, while Sam and Mimi went into the tasting room. Ali paused, wiggled her fingers, and gave Sean an impish smile. "See you later, 'gater!"

He grinned and offered the response the child was clearly waiting for, "After a while, crocodile."

As soon as the door shut, Sean covered the space between him and Megan in three long strides, took her face between his palms, and without a word, kissed her full on the mouth. Too startled to react at first, Megan recovered quickly and wound her arms around his neck, kissing him back, softly at first, then building in urgency until she was lost in his lips and he was lost in her. Heat radiated off his big body pressed to hers as ripples of longing swept over her. His hands roamed over her back, over the bare flesh of her shoulders above the low cut of the yellow silk dress, and back down to her hip.

He gave a frustrated groan and pulled back. "Where's the damn zipper on this thing?" he growled, his eyes glowing with anticipation and purpose.

She placed both hands on his chest. "I can't tell you that."

He lowered his head to that uber-sensitive spot where neck meets shoulder and licked, then whispered, "Why not? I just need to touch you."

Yes, yes, yes, the zipper's on the side. Touch me! she thought, however, she said, "We have to witness your brother and my friend's wedding vows in about twelve minutes, so stop messing me up, Sean Donal Flaherty, and get out of here. I'll follow you in a couple of minutes." But she turned her face up to his so his lips could find hers again.

After one more long, incredible kiss, he released her and gave her a broad wink. "God, I'm glad I taught you to kiss so well back in seventh grade, Meggy."

"*You* taught *me?*" Megan's voice sounded breathless to her own ears and she was trembling. "Um, I'm pretty sure it was the other way around, sparky." She swallowed hard, then batted her eyelashes at him and turned to the full-length mirror on the bathroom door to check how much damage he'd done to her hair and makeup. Not too disarrayed, thank heaven, but her lips were reddened and slightly swollen. She looked thoroughly kissed, no matter who had taught whom all those years ago.

He stepped behind her in the mirror, delicious and masculine in a light blue button-down, tan cotton khakis, and a blue-and-yellow-striped tie. "That's not how I remember it," he murmured. His dark hair, curling over his collar, was longer than she'd seen it since before he graduated law school. The look worked for him, though, with the new trimmed scruff of beard on his jaw. He slid his hands down her bare arms before dropping a kiss on her shoulder. "Megan…" Her name was a breath, warm and caressing.

She gazed at him in the mirror, drowning in the tenderness showing in the blue depths of his eyes. Canting her head, she leaned against his shoulder and pressed her lips to his ear. "Okay, *I'll* go. One of us has to stay sane today. Wipe the lipstick off your face, dude." Sidling around him, she stepped away reluctantly, letting one hand linger on his forearm before she rushed out of the cottage, his deep chuckle following her.

The man is killing me; truly, seriously killing me.

Slightly winded, she made it into the tasting room just as Carly and Bette took their places on either side of Sam. Both women were escorting the bride down the "aisle" that Brendan and Aidan had created with the long white runner they used for weddings at Four Irish Brothers Winery up on the ridge. It flowed over the floor of the low-ceilinged cedar-and-stone building, out the open French doors, down across the top deck, and ended below on the second-level deck at a daisy-covered wire arch Sandy and her crew from Posey Pushers had created. The DJ had set up in one corner of the upper deck, Brendan, Aidan, Joe Samuels—Bette's husband—and Mac sat together at one of the tables near the arch, while Father Mark, the priest from St. Agnes Episcopal Church, stood front and center amidst an array of flowers.

Everyone was ready for the service, except for the maid of

honor and the best man. All three women gave Megan wide eyes as she grabbed her bouquet and stepped in front of them, behind Ali. Turning to Sam, she raised her hands in supplication. "Minor dress emergency," she mouthed, feeling heat flush her cheeks.

Sam eyed her meaningfully before offering an amused gaze. "Sure, Megs. Glad you could make it."

Just then, Sean slipped past them, his limp barely noticeable, as he straightened his tie. He slowed at the steps to avoid stumbling and made his way to the arch to stand next to Conor, who looked relieved, happy, and handsome in tan khakis, a white shirt, and a striped tie that matched Sean's. Certain she'd trip on the runner if she caught his eye, Megan didn't even glance in Sean's direction. Instead, she took a deep breath and stared down at her bouquet of yellow and white daisies.

Sam had deliberately gone low-key and informal for the late-afternoon wedding, so they would be comfortable in the September-in-Indiana heat. Everyone was grateful to be able to dress casually, even though the temperatures were only due to top out in the mid-seventies. Once the rest of the guests arrived for the reception, the venue would be more crowded and warmer; however, the evening breeze coming off the river would keep things bearable.

Sam's own dress was an unpretentious, but elegant, ivory silk street-length slip dress that emphasized her height and showed off her beautiful long legs. Her auburn hair was done in a simple knot at her neck and she, too, wore a flower tiara. She looked so beautiful, even Carly had approved. Carly had borrowed and refitted one of Sam's sundresses for her mother-of-the bride attire since the raw silk suit she'd brought would have been completely inappropriate. The soft cotton dress was the perfect choice and she looked as gorgeous as her daughter. Megan noticed that her dad's eyes were glued to the mother of the bride—something she'd have to think about later.

Ali, who was fidgeting as she waited for the DJ to start the music, suddenly turned around to Sam, consternation clouding her face. "Sam, Da and Uncle Sean have *flip-flops* on! That's not wedding clothes!" She stage-whispered so loudly it brought chuckles from all the adults present.

Sam beamed at her. "I know, honey, but they pouted, so I told them if they bought new leather ones, it would be okay."

Ali rolled her eyes. "Boys," she muttered in five-year-old exasperation, nearly choking Megan, while Sam, Carly, and Bette all snickered.

The music began then—Etta James's version of "At Last," one of Sam's favorite songs, so Ali shrugged and headed up the aisle, scattering yellow rose petals with abandon.

SEAN LOOKED UP from his plate of hors d'oeuvres when Conor and Char joined him and Brendan at their table on the lower deck.

"Where's Aidan?" Char asked as she settled into a chair across from Sean with a sampling of Mac's delicious goodies and an empty glass that Brendan promptly filled with sparkling traminette.

Sean, his mouth full of some kind of amazing smoked salmon thingy on crisp rye toast, lifted his chin toward the edge of the deck, where Aidan stood staring east up the river.

"Conor, have him come join us for a minute, would you?" Char's expression was mysterious—not grim—but it was clear she had something to say and apparently it needed to be said to all four of them.

Sean scanned the decks for Megan, whom he'd pretty much avoided since the ceremony because he was convinced if he got within a foot of her, he'd never be able to keep his hands to himself. Besides, she'd been busy with MOH duties and helping Mac, Carly, and diner servers Norma and Sheila in the small kitchen behind the tasting room. So he'd made the rounds of the guests, accepting warm good wishes from everyone who seemed quite glad to hear he was back home for good.

He spotted her sexy yellow sundress up by the buffet table on the screened porch and watched as she laughed with Harry while she refilled a platter of hors d'oeuvres. Was it nuts to be envious of a seventy-some-odd-year-old man because he was simply laughing with the one woman in the place Sean himself was dying to spirit away and ravish?

"Dude, just go ask her to dance." Brendan drained his glass and refilled it from the bottle on the table. "You've been following her with your eyes since she walked up the aisle. You're being a little obvious."

"All in good time, bro, all in good time." Sean winked and took a sip of wine as Aidan and Conor joined them. He was holding onto the fact that Megan was wearing the string bracelet. That seemed like a good sign. It would've been back in high school.

"You're an idiot, you know that?" Brendan scoffed before turning his attention to Char.

Char folded her hands on the table and took a deep breath. "Boys, I've made a decision. I'm moving to Seaside."

Stunned, Sean set his glass down. Char decamping to Florida was the last thing he expected to hear today and from the expressions on his brothers' faces, with the exception of Conor, they were as shocked as he was. "You're kidding, Char! Is Ethel not doing well?"

Char chuckled. "She's fine. Healed up and amazing the physical therapists down there. Heck, you know Mom. She'll be buzzing around on that damn moped when all of us are either in our graves or at the very least on walkers." She waved a hand dismissively at the notion that fireball Ethel could be having problems. "No, I just think I'd like to be closer to her. In spite of the fact that she's healthy as a horse, she's not going to live forever, and there's a place for rent in a building near Mom's neighborhood that I've looked at and it seems perfect for me."

Conor leaned into the table. "I know we talked about this last night, but are you sure? This is a huge step, Char, and we'll miss you like crazy."

Char patted his arm. "I'll miss you guys, too, but I'm ready to be away from Indiana winters and"—she paused as rosy color filled her cheeks—"well, there's this man down there…"

"A man?" Aidan chortled. "You're in love, Char? That's fantastic!"

Char's blush deepened. "Well, I *could* be, given the chance. He's the orthopedic surgeon who did Mom's hip replacement after her accident. We… we've been seeing quite a lot of each other. He's a widower with three married kids who are all in the area and four grandkids, who are darling."

In spite of the ache in his heart at the fact that Char was leaving just as he was returning, Sean leaped up and came around the table to hug her and plant a kiss on her soft cheek. "Char, that's wonderful! No one deserves love more than you do." He plopped back in his chair while his brothers followed suit, hugging and kissing their stepmother as tears shimmered in her eyes.

She dabbed at her cheeks with a napkin. "I was afraid you boys would think it was too soon after Donal. Frankly,

I'm a little dazed myself, but… but I think Donal would approve."

Brendan nodded. "I'm sure Da would approve, Char. He was a true romantic; he'd want you to be happy." He gave her another quick hug as the others agreed enthusiastically.

"Thanks, Bren." Char smiled through her tears. "Lordy, I'm going to miss you boys so much. I promise I won't go until after Chautauqua, but I've already put a deposit on the condo and Miles is hoping I can spend the holidays with him and his family. That's his name—Dr. Miles Foster. I thought I'd bring him up here for New Year's Eve so you all can meet him." She turned to Conor. "I'm sorry I'm leaving you in a lurch here." She gestured broadly to include the building they currently occupied.

Sean covered her hand with his own. "Don't sweat it, Char. I'll take care of this place—I've been running it while you were gone anyway."

She looked slightly askance. "But I thought Conor said you were going to work with Sam."

"I am, but more important, I'm back to be part of Four Irish Brothers—a part of the legacy Da left us. Besides, I've had a great time working this place while you've been away. You can show me anything I've missed though or special things you do that make it run more smoothly. You know this tasting room like the back of your hand and I'm sure I could use some pointers."

Aidan refilled everyone's glass from the bottles on the

table and then raised his in a toast. "To Char—our mom, our support, our friend. May love and joy be yours as you start this new journey. Know, though, that you always have a home here with us. We love you, sweetheart. *Sláinte.*"

They all clinked glasses and repeated, "*Sláinte.*"

Char didn't even attempt to staunch the flow of tears and Sean's own eyes stung as he tried to imagine Four Irish Brothers Winery without Charlotte Flaherty's strong, steady presence.

Char set her glass down. "I need to powder my nose." She left them on a faint waft of lily of the valley, her signature scent, and one that Sean would forever associate with the woman who'd so lovingly stepped in to fill his mother's shoes all those years ago.

He eyed Conor. "How long have you known about this?"

Conor shook his head, "Just since yesterday afternoon when she got back. She asked me not to say anything. She wanted to tell you guys herself."

Aidan sighed, a huge exhale from the bottom of his lungs as he gazed out over the river. "God, things change fast, don't they?" His voice quavered, sounding remarkably like the little brother Sean remembered from years past.

Sean nudged Aidan with his elbow, aware of how rocket-fast his own life had changed in the past few months. "Change is a part of life, kid, it's all gonna be okay."

Aidan offered up a weak smile. "Maybe." His brow furrowed as he pointed east up the river. "What's up there? Is that the ticket office for the old River Queen showboat?"

Sean, Conor, and Brendan followed where he was pointing, all of them squinting in the evening dusk.

Bren nodded. "Yeah, I think it is. River Queen's been closed for ages though, hasn't it, Con?"

Conor rose, picking up his glass. "Clive Peterson stopped doing shows there not long after you went to college, Ace." He smiled as he ruffled their youngest brother's perfect blond hair. "He lost his best actor, so he ran it as a bar for a while; had quite a floating—if you'll excuse the pun—poker game going on Thursday nights. He died about a year ago, though, and it's been dry-docked since he closed the bar. You can see it there." He aimed one finger just north of the ramshackle hut by the water's edge, pointing out a hulking shape. "Been for sale for a while now, but I don't think anyone's shown any interest."

Aidan chewed his lower lip, a faraway look in his eyes. "What do they want for it?"

When Conor shook his head, a lock of dark hair fell over his forehead. "No clue. Harry would probably know. Why?"

Aidan shrugged. "Just curious. I spent a lot of time on that old tub back in high school doing plays with Clive and his troupe. Kinda sad to see it abandoned. Wondering what became of everyone, that's all."

Conor grinned. "Nothing like a wedding to bring on the sappy memories, huh?" With that he took off, no doubt to retrieve his bride, who was dancing with Joe Samuels. Bren wandered away, too, toward the screened porch and the food and Paula's delicious wedding cake.

Sean watched a myriad of expressions cross Aidan's face and suddenly realized that his baby brother had been unusually subdued all evening. Not melancholy, just quieter than usual. "You okay, Ace?"

Aidan didn't respond at first, then he drained his glass and stood up abruptly. "Yeah. Just remembering old times. Con's right. Weddings make us sappy and you know what? I like sappy, so why don't you go over there and see if you can't get that incredibly hot blonde to pay some attention to you? Who knows what might come of it?"

Chapter Twenty

"NOW THERE'S SOMETHING I never thought I'd see in my lifetime." Sam dropped into a chair across from Megan.

Megan reached for the bottle of traminette on the table, refilled her glass, and started to pour some into the nearly empty glass that Sam had set down, but her friend covered it with her palm. "No, thanks."

Megan eyed her for a moment, then shrugged. "Okay. What did you never think you'd see?"

Sam lifted her chin toward the cake table near the screened porch. "My mother boxing up cake and handing it out to my wedding guests."

Sure enough, Carly and Bette were busily filling yellow individual cake boxes with slices of Paula's amazing pineapple-cream-filled butter cake and passing them to guests as they left. The two older women laughed together as Bette _____ ____ of yellow icing from Carly's cheek just before Sam's mother in a farewell hug.

, leaving pink and orange streaks across ne, probably Sean, had turned on the string lights that crisscrossed the deck from the pergola to the building, the clear vintage-style bulbs giving off a warm glow. The reception was breaking up very slowly as guests lingered over one last glass of sparkling wine or one more dance. The DJ had packed up over an hour ago, but some enterprising soul had Bluetoothed their phone to the wireless speakers, so music still filled the air. Megan suspected it might have been her dad because the songs were oldies from the sixties and seventies—his favorite era of music.

All in all, it had been a perfect wedding, except for the fact that Megan had barely seen or spoken to Sean. Between helping in the kitchen and at the buffet line and taking care of maid-of-honor duties, such as they were, she'd been too busy to take a breath until now.

Sean had stuck close to his brothers, but she'd seen him acting as host, pouring wine and other beverages, helping Aidan and Bren collect empty bottles from the dozen or so tables on the decks, and replacing them with new chilled ones. Seemed like everyone at the reception wanted to catch up with him—every time Megan caught his eye, someone had him cornered. She knew him well enough to know he was deliberately avoiding dancing with her and she didn't blame him.

After the scene in the cottage before the wedding, she was all too aware that being in Sean's arms would set off a series of fireworks she couldn't be sure would stop at a simple dance. His effect on her astounded her. Who could've imagined it a year ago? *How extraordinary!* And yet, in some ways, the delicious spasm of pleasure that coursed through her at the very sight of his brawny frame felt comfortably familiar. She pulled her attention back to Sam.

"Carly sure is a hit with everyone," Megan observed as she and Sam watched Sam's elegant mother engage in a little three-way foxtrot with Clyde and Gloria Schwimmer as she handed them their cake. "Especially my dad."

Mac had just come back to the porch with a stack of clean party-sized chafing dishes he'd clearly meant to load into the back of his truck; however, he'd taken a detour through the porch. Megan grinned as he set the dishes down to cut into the impromptu dance. He twirled Carly around the cake table, then dipped her with such panache that his moves brought a round of applause from those folks waiting for cake.

Sam sighed. "What am I going to do if she decides she's going to stay?"

Megan chuckled. "Give her your apartment and about six more grandkids, 'cause, baby, that woman was born to be a granny."

"I can do that. Ali adores her already." Sam smiled a mysterious little smile. "And more will be along before you know it."

Megan peered at her friend, who was glowing in the lights strung along the pergola and suddenly, she realized that it wasn't just a new bride glow. *Oh. My. God.* "You haven't been drinking wine today, have you? You weren't drinking last night either, come to think of it." She grabbed Sam's glass and took a sip. "Pellegrino in a wineglass. Samantha Hayes Flaherty," she whispered, putting her head close to Sam's. "Are you preggers?"

Sam grinned. "Shh, it's a secret. Only Conor and I know so far. So no discussing it right now."

Megan nearly squealed with delight, but managed to quell her enthusiasm as Sam gave her a warning look. Sipping her own wine, Megan allowed herself a few seconds of wistfulness.

A baby…

Swallowing the lump in her throat, she craned her neck, looking down at the tableful of Flaherty boys on the deck below. "What do you suppose that's about?"

"Char called them all together to tell them she's moving to Florida." Sam took a sip of water and tilted her head back to let the cool evening breeze off the river ruffle the tendrils of auburn hair that had fallen out of her knot.

Megan sat up and slapped her hand on the glass-top table. "You're kidding? Is Ethel okay?"

"She's fine. Char's just ready to move on." Sam sighed. "We're all going to miss her, especially Ali. I'm so glad she's going to stay with her while we're in Aruba. It's only five nights, but they'll have a great time together before Char heads back."

"You two look done in." Wineglasses in hand, Bette and

Carly joined them at the table after the last of the guests had collected their cake boxes and departed. "Anything left in that bottle?" Bette indicated her empty glass with a nod.

Megan obligingly poured them both some wine before emptying the bottle into her own glass. "Where are Dad and Joe?"

"Hauling stuff out to the truck." Carly pulled a chair from another table closer, slipped out of her sandals, and rested her feet in the seat next to her. "All the guests have left, they all got a piece of cake, and we still have cake left over. Char will put your cake top in the freezer at home to save for your first anniversary."

Bette sighed. "And it will taste like crap because a year is way too long to leave cake in the freezer, but eat it anyway because it's tradition." She clinked glasses with Carly. "To tradition."

Carly clinked with her and then turned to Sam. "Samantha, my darling girl, this has been a perfectly lovely wedding. Thank you for allowing me to be a part."

The lump in Megan's throat reappeared as she noticed that Samantha had tears in her eyes when she turned to her mother. "You've been amazing, Mom, thank you. I can't imagine this day without you."

Carly grinned, her perfect white teeth gleaming in the string lights. "I've had the time of my life this week." She glanced up as Mac and Joe came back through the tasting room with another load of equipment from the kitchen. "I almost hate to leave." The words were so quiet, Megan wasn't even sure she'd heard Carly correctly.

Suddenly, Sam leaned forward and took her mother's hand. "Then don't. Stay. What are you going back to Chicago for anyway?"

Carly offered a pensive smile. "I have commitments there. The symphony board. The hospital board. My building's board…"

"I think your daughter is asking you to move closer to her, Carly." Bette nudged Carly's shoulder gently. "What board is more important than that?"

When Carly looked at Sam in wonder, Sam nodded. "I am, Mom. You can have my apartment. Meg and I were just talking about it."

Megan gaped, she couldn't help it. *Holy crap!* Was Sam actually *asking* her mother to move to River's Edge?

Carly's eyes filled. "Oh, Samantha, there's nothing I'd love more than to be closer to you and your family, and"— she bit her lip and gazed around at the tasting room, the river, the deepening navy of the sky, and Graham Mackenzie toting another load of chafing dishes past them—"this place is… magical."

Sam smiled, tears shimmering on her cheeks. "Stay, Mom, please."

Carly rose and put her arms around her daughter. "Let me think about it. I told Char I'd help her with Ali, so I'll be here when you get home from your honeymoon. We both need to sleep on this one; we can talk about it when you get back."

"Talk about what?" Mac appeared behind Megan's chair, setting his hands on her shoulders and massaging gently as she moaned in appreciation.

"What you and Joe intend to feed Carly and me for a late supper." Bette stood up and put one arm around Joe, who'd come out onto the deck with Mac. "How about we try that pub in town? What's it called?" She turned to Mac. "You know, the historic one."

Mac grinned. "Hutchin's House," he said and then intoned, "the oldest continuously running restaurant and tavern on the Ohio River. Or we can go back to my place and I can cook."

Bette shook her head. "Nope. I think you've done enough cooking today, sir. Let's go to the tavern. Our treat."

Mac patted Megan's shoulder and dropped a kiss on her cheek before offering his hand to Carly, who'd already put her shoes back on and was draining her wineglass. "Shall we, Ms. Hayes?"

"I'd be delighted, Mr. Mackenzie." She accepted his hand, her cheeks rosy either from wine or pleasure. Megan suspected it was a little of both.

Just then Conor ambled up and he and Sam began the round of hugs and farewells with her mother and her aunt. Char joined in with Ali in tow and Megan's heart squeezed just a bit as the little girl held on to Sam for dear life.

"Sam, are you and Da really going away?" Ali's lip trembled.

Sam sat back down and tugged Ali onto her lap. "Yes, you know we are, sweetie, but just for a few days. Remember what Da and I told you about honeymoons?"

Ali nodded, glancing up at Conor who was clearly having a tough time keeping a straight face. "I know." The pout became more evident. "It's a special trip that people take right after they get married. But, why can't I go, too?"

"Because honeymoons are just for grown-ups, poppet." Conor knelt next to Sam's chair.

"I don't want you to go away." The tears in Ali's eyes ran down her cheeks.

"We'll be back in five days." Conor brushed at her face with his thumb.

"What if you don't come back? What if you decide to move to A... A..." She choked on the word.

"Aruba?" Sam peered at her new stepdaughter. "Honey, this is only a vacation. Da and I would never move to Aruba. Why would you think such a thing?"

Ali sniffed. "G-Grammy Char went away and n-now she's moving to Florida." She looked up accusingly at Char, whose eyes had widened. "I heard you tell Da yesterday."

All the adults seemed to catch their breath in unison. Megan frowned at the mysteries of literal child logic and was anxious to see how Sam fielded Ali's fears.

Sam hugged Ali close and kissed the top of her head before stroking a tangle of curls off the little girl's tear-stained cheek. "Ali, Grammy Char *is* moving to Florida because she needs to go down to help her mommy, and you can ask her all about that later, okay? Right now, understand that Da and I are coming home in *five days* and we'll all three be living together in your house."

Ali's wet eyes grew round as saucers. "And you're going to live with Da and me forever?"

Sam grinned. "I am."

"Can Mimi come and live with us, too?" Ali eyed Carly, who threw back her head and laughed.

"Slow down, baby girl." Carly extended her hand to Ali. "I've already agreed to stay a week longer so I can help Grammy Char get you ready to start kindergarten. We thought we'd go to Cincinnati for a couple of days to shop for school clothes and—"

"Oh, oh, that's where the aquarium is!" Ali jumped off Sam's lap. "Can we go and see the sharks?"

Carly looked at Char. "What do you think, Grammy Char? Sharks and school clothes?"

Char chuckled and picked Ali up in her arms. "Sharks and school clothes sound perfect. But now, miss, it's time to get you home for a bath and bedtime."

After several more hugs, Carly, Mac, Bette, and Joe trooped out of the tasting room behind Char and Ali, while in the circle of Conor's arms, Sam dabbed at her eyes with a napkin.

Megan blinked at Ali's turnaround from tears to smiles merely at the mention of sharks. Children were indeed a mystery, one she found more and more fascinating as she got older. "That kid is a hoot."

"She is that," Conor agreed, pressing a kiss to Sam's temple. "Okay, gorgeous, I think we've done it all—vows, first kiss, cake, toasts, pictures, dancing, bouquet tossing..." He ticked the items off on his fingers.

Sam kissed him soundly, before turning to hug Megan. "I gotta tell you, Megs, I love that Dot caught the bouquet, even though I was kinda hoping it would be you!"

Megan snickered. "I tried, but she's damn fast for a woman in her fifties. Besides, I've noticed Noah wearing a path between the quilt shop and his hardware store lately, so maybe the right person did catch it."

"Let's get going. Our bags are in the car and our driver has arrived." Conor nodded to Aidan who was just sauntering up with Brendan and Sean.

"Bren, want to ride along?" Aidan offered, dangling Conor's SUV keys in front of his brother's face.

"No, thanks. I thought I'd walk over to the firehouse and take some cake to Tierney. She had to split early because she's on shift." Brendan scrutinized his youngest brother. "Are you good to drive?"

Aidan waved him off. "Oh, yeah. I knew I'd be chauffeuring tonight, so I've only had two glasses of wine all day, and I just finished a cup of coffee with another piece of cake, so I'm all good."

"You sure?" Sean raised one dark brow and Megan was struck at how much alike Bren, Conor, and Sean were in how they looked after their little brother.

Aidan gave them a patronizing smile. "We can call Duane and have him bring his breathalyzer over if it would make you all feel better." Then he fake staggered and grabbed Sam around her waist. "Lesh go, baby..." He slurred in a perfect imitation of a guy bombed on his ass.

Laughing and teasing, they all tumbled out of the tasting room, and when she looked around, Megan realized that she and Sean were finally alone.

Chapter Twenty-One

THE LENGTHENING SHADOWS covered the view of the river so all that was visible were the lights twinkling on the Kentucky side as Sean gazed across the water. He was trembling. *Trembling!* He took a deep breath before he turned to Megan, who stood in the middle of the upper deck where earlier they'd pushed back tables to clear a dance floor.

"Alone at last." His voice sounded husky and raw to his own ears. "I thought this thing would never end."

Megan smiled and his world tilted. "It's only nine o'clock, Sean."

He glanced through the window behind her at the wine-cork clock hanging on the wall inside the tasting room. So it was. It seemed much later. There was no moon, but stars had begun to appear in the clear night sky and the string lights created a dappled glow on her beautiful face. Every muscle in his body tightened. Dear Lord, all he wanted was to make love to her, right there on the deck and then in the tasting room and then in the cottage, and maybe by that time, he'd have satisfied his hunger enough to take her home to bed.

He stepped closer to her and paused. "Don't go anywhere, I'll be right back."

"Where are you going?"

"Just to lock up. Don't move." He limped to the front of the tasting room and locked the door, leaving the CLOSED FOR PRIVATE EVENT sign in place before switching off the lights in the little wine-tchotchkes shop that was the entrance to the Four Irish Brothers Winery's in-town tasting room. A mistake, as it turned out, because he bumped into a rack of decorative stoppers and other wine paraphernalia in his rush to get back to Megan. But he didn't want anyone to come knocking and interrupt them. Not tonight.

When he came back, a little breathless from grabbing the rack before it fell over, Megan stood by the deck rail, gazing out at the red, green, and white lights of a passing barge. Her bare shoulders gleamed peachy pink in the lights from above and again, longing arced through him.

She glanced back at him. "Looks like a coal barge."

A rather inane remark, which made Sean wonder if she was as nervous as him, in spite of her serene smile, but before he had a chance to consider the possibility any further, she turned, her arms crossed over her breasts as she met his eyes. "Sam told me about Char moving to Florida. I know you'll all miss her, but you probably most of all since you've been living with her a good bit of the summer."

Ah, small talk. So that was how they were going to play it. He could go along for a few minutes.

He nodded and stepped closer, so close he picked up that

unique delicate scent that was his Meg—flowers and peaches and a faint hint of... was it something citrus? Whatever it was, it intoxicated him. "Yup, Con says she's going to make arrangements with movers next week and probably be gone right after Chautauqua. We are going to miss her, but it's a good thing for her—moving on, starting a new life."

Megan pinned him with her gaze. "Seems to be a lot of that going around River's Edge lately. Why didn't you tell me that you were moving back for good?"

Sean smiled. Okay, so no small talk because this was Meg and Meg always got right to the heart of any situation. "I *did* tell you. But you didn't believe me. I'm home, Megan." He took one more step toward her, but kept his hands at his side. "And not because I'm afraid of Chicago or because my head is messed up from the shooting. This has been on my mind since before Sam came down here last year."

She held out a hand. "Sean, don't. I'm sorry I—"

He touched one finger to her full lips, then dropped his hand before he lost the small grip he had on his self-control. Touching her now would blow his whole plan. "Shh. Let me finish."

Blinking, she took one step back and gave him a brief nod.

"The shooting was just the catalyst for a move I've needed—no, *wanted*—to make for at least the last two years. I want to be here, to be a part of the winery, to be with my family. It's what I've been dreaming about, but couldn't seem to make happen. When I woke up in the hospital and saw you there…" He struggled with the words, needing exactly the correct ones, the words that would make her see. Make her understand. "It was *right*, Meg—you being by my hospital bed made perfect sense in a time and place where nothing at all made sense."

She offered him the same sad little smile he'd seen on her face the night before he went back to Chicago. "I know. I was familiar—something to grasp onto when your world turned upside down." She shrugged. "I was safe."

"Would you please stop saying that?" He released an exasperated breath at her wary expression. "I love you, Megan, and it's *not* about needing you to take care of me." He could see she wasn't hearing him, so he repeated the words, "I love you. We have history, and okay, if that means you're *safe*, so be it. What's wrong with safe, Megs? Safe is sexy and comfortable. I want *you* to feel safe with *me*, too."

Tears shimmered in her brandy-colored eyes and his heart wrenched. "Safe *is* good," she said. "So is history. But what if it's not enough? I don't want you to love me just because I'm safe and familiar. That's why you love Char or your brothers or this town."

Tamping down his urgent need, he took her by the shoulders, careful not to let his fingers bite into her soft flesh. "How about if I also love you because you're warm and smart and funny and sexy and beautiful and the best damn company I've ever known—*ever*?"

Her lower lip quivered and she looked so lost, so vulnerable he gave up on words and kissed her. A tender kiss into which he put all the feelings that had been simmering in him since he'd awakened after the shooting. He tasted salt, so he pulled his mouth from her lips to kiss the tears from her cheeks. Framing her face in his palms, he touched his forehead to hers. "Don't you see, Meggy? It's always been you. *Always.* Nothing is real until I've talked about it with you. We're two halves of a whole, we always have been. We're just late discovering it, that's all."

When she pressed against him, he felt the acceleration of her heart against his chest and wondered if the violent knocking of his own heart was fear or hope. When she laughed and kissed him, opening her lips to his, he realized it was joy. Pure, unadulterated *ecstasy.*

MEGAN LOOPED HER arms around Sean's neck as his mouth ravaged hers—somehow, she couldn't seem to get close enough to him. His hands roamed slowly over her back, finding the bare skin of her shoulder blades and stroking, touching each knob of her spine, all the way to her waist, almost as though he was memorizing the shape of her.

"I love you, too, Sean. I've always loved you," she whispered between kisses. "You are my high-water mark."

He pulled back, a question in his navy-blue eyes. "I-I'm

your *what*? What does that mean?"

She touched the scruff of beard on his jaw, then ran her thumb over his full lower lip. "You are the man every other man got compared to, and they all failed the test. I'd think, he's not smart enough or he's not kind enough or he's not funny enough; but what I was really thinking was *he's not Sean.*"

He chuckled and pressed his lips to her forehead. "Funny. It's been the same for me—even in high school. I could never figure out why every time I had a date, I had to call you afterward and rehash the whole miserable experience." He rubbed his cheek on hers, tickling her with his beard. "Remember? We'd end up on the phone, talking for hours?"

A shiver coursed through her as she recalled all the Friday nights she spent lying in bed waiting for his call, telling herself she hoped his date went well, but knowing in her heart, she really hoped it was awful.

He ran his hands down her arms and then tugged her against him again. "It was supposed to be you—every time, every date. It *should* have been you," he murmured, his warm breath stirring the curls over her ears. Suddenly, he released her. "Come here." He took her hand and pulled her over to a chair. "Sit. Stay."

Megan giggled. "Sit? Stay? Do you want me to raise my paw and shake?"

He chuckled and dropped a kiss on the top of her head. "Not yet. Don't move, okay? I'll be right back."

Megan shook her head, still reeling from his kisses and aching for more—for all of him. How had she missed this for so many years? Regret niggled at her mind for all the times she'd thought *if only he were more like Sean* about a date and yet never connected that every other guy ought to have been Sean. She wished she could rewrite the last twenty-five years so they hadn't lost so much time together.

Mère's voice echoed in her brain, the words she'd whispered in Megan's ear at Orly Airport in March when Meg was leaving after having had spent two glorious weeks in Paris with her, *pas de regrets, ma chère fille, Restez dans l'ici et maintenant.*

No regrets. Stay in the here-and-now.

Her mother had preached those words for as long as Megan could remember, reminding her to always find her joy in the present. It was scary—the present. Yet this summer, it seemed as if the world had paused for a moment, giving her and Sean a chance to catch up, to find one another again as friends and much more.

Sean reappeared as the first notes of a song she recognized all too well wafted from the speakers. The first strains of Survivor's "The Search Is Over" began as he carefully knelt on his good knee in front of her and grinned. "Okay, *now* I'll take your paw." He grasped her left hand and pressed a kiss into her palm. "Got a question for you."

Megan flushed with heat as her heart pounded, sure he was going to ask her to move in with him, but not nearly so certain what her answer would be. What would the town think of their mayor living in sin with one of the hot wine-makers from up on the ridge? "Okay?"

His eyes glistened, his voice was husky with emotion. "What are you doing for the next sixty years? Want to spend them with me?" In the fingers of his other hand, a three-stone diamond ring glinted in the lights. "Three stones, past, present, and future. We already share one of them. Say you'll marry me so we can share the other two." He swallowed hard and blinked. "'Tis always been *us*, Meggy. And it always should be." His nervous, unconscious brogue lent magic to his words.

Her breath came faster and her heart skipped a beat or two at the earnestness of his expression. *Marry him?* That wasn't the question she was expecting. For a long moment she gazed at him, his love for her shining like a beacon on his face.

Out of the corner of her eye, she imagined she glimpsed the ghost of her seventeen-year-old self, giving her a smug smile and a nod. Suddenly, everything became clear. *He* was her here-and-now and her future—she belonged with Sean, right here in in this place they both knew so well, working together and maybe even raising up a couple of new Flahertys to help carry on Donal's legacy or to become mayor of River's Edge one day. Sam had been right all along—one way or another, they were destined to be sisters.

She chuckled in pure delight as exhilaration surged

through her. "Yes, I'll marry you, Sean Flaherty," she said grinning through happy tears. "Tonight if you like."

Sean slid the ring onto her finger, kissed her soundly, then slowly got to his feet, pulled her out of her chair, and drew her into his arms. "Ah, Meggy, me darlin', we can wait until tomorrow. I've been dyin' to hold you all day. Right now, let's dance."

The End

Dear Readers,

Authors are notorious for falling in love with their characters and I'm no exception. I have such a great time writing the dialogue between the Flaherty brothers, and often I wish I could spend just an afternoon being a part of this family.

Another reason learning to know the Flaherty brothers has been such fun is that telling their stories gives me a chance to explore two of my very favorite things (besides handsome Irishmen)—food and wine. I'm a true foodie, but I confess I'm not always certain about what wines go with what foods.

As I was writing Sean and Megan's story, I began to think wouldn't it be cool to be able to go down to Four Irish Brothers Winery and talk wine and food pairings with Conor and Sean, and even to have Chef Mac Mackenzie there, too? He is the ultimate foodie in these books and okay, I admit it, I'm crazy in love with that old silver fox.

Maybe the conversation would go a little bit like this:

Nan: Guys, thanks so much for inviting me down, I'm excited to learn about what kinds of foods go with Indiana wines.

Sean: Our pleasure, Nan.

Conor: We love it when folks stop by to talk food and wine because that means Mac will be bringing some fantastic stuff to eat.

Mac: I'm just here for the wine.

Nan: Mac, everything looks amazing. You know, you find all kinds of articles about pairings in foodie magazines, but I really want to talk Indiana wines because I do love exploring all the great wineries here in our state. For instance, traminette, the official grape of Indiana. You guys do something really special with that crisp white wine by making it a sparkling wine.

Conor: Traminette is actually the last wine we're going to taste today, so we'll get to it, I promise. We're tasting four wines—two reds and two whites. Three are Indiana grapes and one is a grape we imported from California. Here's the first one. It's our new zinfandel, Teacher's Pet, which we make with grapes that I bought from a vineyard in the Dry Creek area of Sonoma County in California. We are delighted with how it turned out, and even though it's going to get better as it ages in the bottle, it drinks just fine now.

Sean: One of the things we love about using old-vine California grapes is not only are they very drinkable when we bottle the wine, but they're also holding up in aging. There's a little controversy over whether or not these California zins age well. I've had some California zins that didn't hold up past five to seven years and I've had some that are still great after ten or fifteen years. So, who knows? We're holding a good thought for this one.

Nan: This is delicious. Big and bold fruit, great pepper at the end. It doesn't taste green at all.

Conor: Thanks. I'm hoping it won't fade on us. It shouldn't.

Nan: Mac, what are we pairing with this one?

Mac: Okay, zin is really happy when you pair it with meat, so I've got some barbecued baby back ribs, chili in the little cup there, and aged, smoked Gouda on crisp crackers. Zin works great with dark chocolate too, so here are some miniature dark chocolate brownie bites.

Nan: You just said the magic word! Chocolate! This barbecue sauce is different. Is it possible I'm tasting...um...apples?

Mac: Nan, you have a great palate! It's my own recipe. I use apple butter from Dykeman's Orchard in this sauce. Spicy and sweet.

Sean: Next is the wine we're pretty much famous for on the Wine Trail—chambourcin. It's also known in the east as Pennsylvania zinfandel, but everyone's take on it is different.

Nan: Gotta confess, guys, I'm not a huge chambourcin fan because I just can't get past the slate taste.

Conor: Try this. It's one that our dad made a few years ago before he passed away, and we're down to like three cases, so it's off the tasting menu now, but I wanted *you* to taste it with Mac's cooking. Da took this one in more of a fruity pinot direction, although the earthiness is still there. I'm hoping the one we just put into barrels is going to be as good.

Sean: Mac, what have you got for the chambourcin?

Mac: I've got bacon-wrapped figs stuffed with goat cheese, and on the toothpicks, smoked sausage bites that we're going to dip in this amazing applesauce. I know that sounds weird, but try it. The applesauce has cloves, nutmeg, and cinnamon—gives the grilled sausage a special taste. And again chocolate is on deck—try one of those truffles. They're from Tomlinson's Confections, an Indiana chocolatier down the river apiece.

Nan: I'm in heaven! Bacon, figs, and chocolate all on one plate with, okay, you got me, one of the most amazing chambourcins I've ever tasted. It really is good, you guys, earthy, but fabulous fruit.

Conor: Ah ha! We converted you! Now you'll have a more open mind about chambourcin when you go around tasting at other Midwest wineries.

Sean: Next up is our newest white—gewürztraminer. Its origins are actually in Alsace, France, and the grapes are a little hard to grow here. But we've had good weather the past couple of years and they've done well for us. This gewürztraminer is a big hit with our customers because we make it in between dry and semi-sweet. Whether you like dry whites or sweet ones, this works for almost everybody's palate. Mac, what are you pairing with it?

Mac: Okay, I've got sea bass fish tacos with some medium-spicy salsa, baked Brie on rye toast, and cheesecake bites with apricot compote.

Nan: This is amazing. I love fish tacos, but I've never had sea bass fish tacos before.

Conor: Okay, Nan, here's our last wine—your sparkling traminette, which was our dad's creation originally, but our customers fell in love with it and we can hardly keep it in the store.

Sean: It is a fantastic celebration wine. We always toast the New Year in with it.

Conor: Mac, what have you made to go with the sparkling traminette?

Mac: We've got pork tenderloin sliders with garlic-avocado aioli, Portobello mushroom ravioli, and lobster rolls with a mild pineapple salsa. You don't want a lot of spicy food with this wine because you'll lose the sparkle. It's also great with these sugar cookies and spice cake petit fours.

Sean: Man this pork is delicious! Nice, job, Mac!

Nan: This has been amazing. Guys, thank you so much for the wine and the food—I feel so much smarter about pairings now and I will be back very soon!

Dearest Readers, I hope you had fun with this little imaginary trip to River's Edge and Four Irish Brothers Winery. Traveling to new places and experiencing new things is the best part of being a reader, don't you think? Thanks for coming along with me!

My Very Best Always,
Nan

If you enjoyed this book, please leave a review at your favorite online retailer! Even if it's just a sentence or two it makes all the difference.

Thanks for reading *Meant to Be* by Nan Reinhardt!

Discover your next romance at TulePublishing.com.

TULE
PUBLISHING

If you enjoyed *Meant to Be*, you'll love the next book in….

The Four Irish Brothers Winery series

Book 1: *A Small Town Christmas*

Book 2: *Meant to Be*

Book 3: *A Showboat Christmas*

Available now at your favorite online retailer!

About the Author

Nan Reinhardt has been a copy editor and proofreader for over twenty-five years, and currently works mainly on fiction titles for a variety of clients, including Avon Books, St. Martin's Press, Kensington Books, Tule Publishing, and Entangled Publishing, as well as for many indie authors.

Author Nan writes romantic fiction for women in their prime. Yeah, women still fall in love and have sex, even after they turn forty-five! Imagine! She is also a wife, a mom, a mother-in-law, and a grandmother. She's been an antiques dealer, a bank teller, a stay-at-home mom, and a secretary.

She loves her career as a freelance editor, but writing is Nan's first and most enduring passion. She can't remember a time in her life when she wasn't writing—she wrote her first romance novel at the age of ten, a love story between the most sophisticated person she knew at the time, her older sister (who was in high school and had a driver's license!), and a member of Herman's Hermits. If you remember who they are, *you* are Nan's audience! She's still writing romance, but now from the viewpoint of a wiser, slightly rumpled, post-menopausal woman who believes that love never ages, women only grow more interesting, and everybody needs a little sexy romance.

Thank you for reading

Meant to Be

If you enjoyed this book, you can find more from all our great authors at TulePublishing.com, or from your favorite online retailer.

TULE
PUBLISHING

57136488R00163

Made in the USA
Middletown, DE
27 July 2019